The Purposeful Oliver Burke

Will Appiah

The Purposeful Oliver Burke

First print

This book is a dedication to everyone who was taken from us before they had a chance to execute their dream. Your vision of creating a better tomorrow will continue to live through the lives of everyone you touched.

Table of Contents

CHAPTER 1:
JOB WELL DONE, SIR 1
CHAPTER 2:
KAROT 14
CHAPTER 3:
BROKEN MIRRORS 22
CHAPTER 4:
I WILL ALWAYS PROTECT YOU 33
CHAPTER 5:
TRUST ISSUES 45
CHAPTER 6:
THE MOMENTS WE KNEW 53
CHAPTER 7:
THINGS WE FIGHT FOR 69
CHAPTER 8:
THE HILLS HAVE EYES 78
CHAPTER 9:
BEST LIFE 90
CHAPTER 10:
11TH FLOOR 98
CHAPTER 11:
REASONS WE CARE 111
CHAPTER 12:
LOVE YOU FROM A DISTANCE 122
CHAPTER 13:
MOMENTS IN TIME WHEN THE CLOCK STOPS 128
CHAPTER 14:
THE PEOPLE WE COULD NOT SAVE 145
CHAPTER 15:
DON'T LOOK BACK 152
CHAPTER 16:
BORN HEROES 159
CHAPTER 17:
"LOVE, J." 168
CHAPTER 18:
"HOW HAVE I WRONGED YOU?" 179
CHAPTER 19:
THE JOVIAL GIANT 191

CHAPTER 20:
THE EARLIEST BIRD IN BATON ROUGE 202
CHAPTER 21:
#GRADUATION 213
CHAPTER 22:
WE WILL NOT WASTE YOUR PAIN 226
CHAPTER 23:
EIGHT LEVELS OF CHARITY 236
CHAPTER 24:
YOU SAVED MY LIFE..249

"When people get touched, they light up. When they don't, they go into the shadows."

- *Richard Branson*

The Purposeful Oliver Burke

PART I
AKWAABA

CHAPTER 1:

JOB WELL DONE, SIR

Present Day- January 2016

In the vibrant borough of Manhattan, attendees gathered in Bryant Park that winter evening to celebrate and raise funds for youth programs. The temperature was just below twenty degrees Fahrenheit and the light snowfall made NYC a beautiful place to be. Large banners hung on both the 42nd Street and the Avenue of the Americas entrances, which were used to welcome attendees and attract anyone passing by. The banners read "Skate and Sip: A Fundraiser for Our Future," which spoke to the event's focus of raising funds for the United Way NYC. They were at the tail end of their winter children's campaign and this event was the organization's final effort to raise money. While everyone was invited, the main demographics the organizers focused on were young professionals, philanthropists, and parents and their children. Presale tickets for this event began just days before Christmas and had continued to be bought right into this year.

Most of the ticket presales came from individuals who fell within one of the three groups, but as time went on, organizers saw tickets being sold in batches to many corporations who were looking to fulfill their commitment to social responsibility and corporate citizenship. Three years earlier, a partnership of not-for-profit organizations in Manhattan was formed to align resources, share networks and partner with local businesses. The newly formed coalition helped all participating organizations remain in sync with each other's activities while working toward similar goals. This accountability helped leaders from each of these groups stay honest and informed, while helping members stay connected.

The event was proving to be successful. Based on ticket presales alone, the United Way was already at a 115% return on its investment. Most food vendors donated their time and cuisine for the cause.

But what really made this fundraiser so successful was that it was after the New Year's holiday. The holiday season was one of New York City's busiest times of the year and after the season was over, most business and hospitality outlets began their slow period which allowed them the time to help a good cause.

Despite the holiday season officially ending a few days prior, the city was still illuminated with Christmas lights and decorations. This made Bryant Park look like a winter wonderland and provided the holiday stragglers an opportunity to see the city's decorations while avoiding the crowds. Most people were just returning to work after their time off so organizers knew this was the perfect opportunity to host this type of fundraiser.

As the event got underway, the snow slowed down to almost nothing. Attendees chatted while the wait staff circled the park with finger food and napkins. Multiple food vendors volunteered to cater the fundraiser for free in hopes of benefitting from the exposure. The event's attendees took full advantage of this and were enjoying the wide variety of free food. Most of the walk-up booths had lines of people waiting, and the line for the open bar was just as long as the lines for food stands.

As children ice skated, parents happily monitored while smiling and waving from a distance. The DJ was playing hits off the current top 20 playlist which attracted people passing by. There were lots of people in the park, but still plenty of space to move around and network.

About midway through the event, an elderly lady got on stage and began to ask for the crowd's attention. She introduced herself as Susan Hedgeland, chairperson of United Way NY. She started by thanking everyone for coming to the evening's fundraiser and then spoke a little bit about the organization and its mission. She announced the raffles would be closing in a few minutes and encouraged the attendees to pull those final few dollars from the bottom of their wallets and purses. Susan then began speaking about ways the attendees could help them push their mission forward by signing up to volunteer at other events, and encouraged the crowd to serve as ambassadors, spreading their mission.

After her speech, Susan welcomed Walter Benine, the board's newly elected vice chair, to the stage. In her introduction, she told the audience that he will speak to them about the board's involvement with the coalition, and how the United Way board and Non-Profit Coalition partner with the city of Manhattan.

Before he began, Walter asked for the waitstaff to pass beverages around and ensure everyone in the crowd had a drink. "My name is Walter Benine, and I am proud to serve the United Way as Vice Chair of the organization and Chair of the NYC Non-Profit Coalition. I was very withdrawn as a child, which caused me to stay away from other kids. Before I became the Walter Benine you see in front of you, I was described as a strange loner. I know it may seem surprising since I probably strike you as a confident, leader, but that wasn't always the case. It didn't hurt me because I saw others as judgmental monsters who wanted to hurt me, and I didn't need them in my life to be happy. As a result, in my early preteen years, I did not have many friends. It wasn't until I received a helping hand from someone I had shunned that I realized isolating myself was doing nothing for me except leaving me to fight the real monsters alone.

"To me, our coalition represents the building blocks to equipping these organizations with the tools they need to provide for those in need. This is especially important for children in need. All of our organizations have the vision but some may lack the network and resources to fulfill their commitments to those in need. To achieve our goals, we must continue to apply discipline and consistency. We will continue to move forward as long as we continue to have friends and supporters like you. I'd like to ask each person here to raise your glass whether it's filled with champagne, liquor, hot chocolate or apple juice. Please raise your glasses and help me celebrate all of you for taking a grand step forward with us. Salud!"

Walter turned and handed the microphone to the next speaker, who began announcing the raffle winners. As he exited the stage after his speech, Susan walked over to Walter and shook his hand.

"Job well done, sir."

"Thank you, Susan."

Walter allowed Susan to lead him over to a small group, where she presented him to three individuals who were silent donors to the organization. She introduced the two elderly, white women as Mrs. Rose Jacobs and Mrs. Lucy Harrison. She then introduced Walter to a middle aged, heavyset African American man, Eugene Garry. The individuals told Walter what a great job he did and praised his accomplishments with both organizations.

Eugene told Walter what an impact this type of event has on him, because he has two young children and one of them has muscular dystrophy. He would hate for her to grow up in a world that counts her out before she has a chance to be great. He also wanted her to have the confidence to know she can be great despite any circumstance. Eugene said he was happy to partner with United Way and that he would like to work with Walter more in the future. He told Walter that he, too, worked in Manhattan, and would like to get together with him one day. He commented on how impressed he was with Walter's presentation and demeanor, an observation to which Mrs. Harrison flirtatiously agreed. Eugene ended his conversation with Walter by making a joke about how it looked like the women in the crowd enjoyed Walter's speech the best, which a bashful Walter laughed off.

As the group made its way back to the bar, Walter received an email from his company's talent office, titled *Performance Bonus—Submission Complete.* This came as a surprise to Walter, because he had never received this type of email before. As he read the email, he noticed it mentioned the client he signed a few days prior. After reading the email further, Walter was pleasantly surprised to see that the letter detailed his performance and contribution to the recent signing. It also spoke about the role his team played in the process. He did not expect anything for doing his job, but was delighted to see his efforts recognized.

As the event came to a close, Walter began walking toward the Herald Square PATH train station to head home. He crossed, and continued to walk down Avenue of the Americas toward 33rd Street. As he crossed 40th Street, Walter saw an old man dressed all in black standing at a bus stop full of people. The man had a long white beard, a baseball cap and glasses perched on his nose. He stood with a cart full of miscellaneous items and stared aimlessly at the street. Walter was confused, because the man didn't look homeless, nor was he asking anyone for anything. Instead, he just stood there with a blank look on his face as if deep in thought. He looked like he may be waiting for the bus, or maybe he was lost.

Passing by, Walter walked directly behind the man and braced himself for the awful smell that always accompanied the city's displaced persons. Surprisingly, he smelled nothing. This confused Walter, but he continued walking toward his destination. After reaching the end of the block, something compelled Walter to stop. Something about the situation didn't feel right. Something in him made him feel the need to turn around, so he did. He began to walk back toward the man and while walking, he reached in his pocket, grabbing whatever cash was there and gripping it in his hand. When he reached the man, he extended a hand full of cash for a handshake. The man looked from Walter's hand to his eyes, then extended his hand.

As they shook hands, Walter passed the cash to the man. The elderly man looked down at his hand and back up at Walter. While their hands were still locked, he pulled Walter in closer and in a very soft voice, he asked Walter his name.

"My name is Walter Benine," Walter replied.

The elderly man replied by whispering his own name, which Walter was unable to hear because of the softness in his voice.

The old man then asked, "Why did you walk over to me?"

"I don't know, but something made me turn around."

"Interesting. I can sense you're a very strong and caring individual with a pure heart," remarked the old man. There is kindness in your eyes and a fullness in your heart. I see a sense of satisfaction in your face but also emptiness and regret. I don't see a fully broken mirror but it looks like there are some cracks in the image you see of yourself. Without prying too deeply, I'd say you've recently been hurt by something, or questioned yourself. Am I wrong in that assumption?"

Just then, the bus pulled up and the passengers began boarding. Before Walter could answer the question, the old man smiled and began walking toward the entrance of bus.

Stunned by what the man said, Walter stared speechless as the man walked away. Shaking his head to clear his mind, he yelled, "Wait! I haven't been hurt by anything…but I'd like to talk more."

"You will learn more when the time is right." With that, the old man boarded the bus.

As he walked away, Walter realized how confusing the whole thing was. He told himself that he did not have anything he regretted, nor did he feel empty inside. He wasn't entirely sure what the old man was referring to.

I am successful in my dream career, can date any woman I want and the nonprofit organizations that I am aligned with just hosted a successful event tonight. That old man has no idea what he was saying.

His mind was troubled though, as he continued to walk toward the train station.

In his professional career, Walter worked as a digital associate director for a top ten advertising agency that specialized in commercials, billboards and social media marketing. In his role, he worked within the client markets sector, which focused on client relationship management.

Since joining the team, Walter was able to make some changes to his roster and build a strong team. His strategic acumen and developmental approach helped ensure he was able to construct a high-performing team. He was known as one of strongest closers within the agency, and he wanted to make sure his team achieved the same reputation. His ability to make contracts out of nothing had helped him achieve success within the industry. He was also skilled in helping clients understand how much value they could get with his agency supporting more than just the client's marketing. He wanted each client to view the agency as their advocate on anything technology-related. When he joined, he told himself that he wanted to create a relationship that was more than just transactional. His goal was to create a working relationship that was memorable.

Walter's theory was that most businesses that sought our marketing support didn't know what they needed until you told them how others have benefited from saying yes to signing with the Karot Agency. This was a strategy that helped him land some of the industry's biggest and most important deals. Another major factor of his success at the agency was based on how many clients he could get to renew and re-sign a contract before it expired. It was almost as if he knew which clients would renew when he got them to sign the original contract.

Walter loved his responsibility at Karot, and took a particular interest in maintaining client relationships. He loved everything about his current clients and the onboarding aspect of new clients.

Receiving the email tonight was a reminder that he was excelling and this made him happy. He had invested so much of himself into his work, and seeing the fruits of his labors was important.

*****

A few weeks after the Skate & Sip event, Walter received more confirmation that he was excelling in his career. One Monday morning in late February, as Walter exited the elevator on his office floor, the entire room erupted in cheers. He assumed this may be a prank until various colleagues approached Walter to congratulate him.

When he asked a colleague what he was being congratulated for, they jokingly replied, "For ensuring we'll have jobs at the end of the year."

Walter's boss then walked up to him with his arms wide open and told him that the two contracts they were bidding for had finally been signed, and congratulates him. He stated that Walter and his team were responsible for the signing of three multimillion-dollar contracts to the agency in the first quarter of the year.

A shocked Walter smiled. He'd spent so much time focusing on the new contract he just signed at the start of the year, he almost forgot he had re-negotiated two other contracts right before the new year. He was happy to hear that both clients decided to continue to do business with the agency. He knew that signing a new big client while re-signing two of their other biggest clients would help him create his legacy at the agency.

As Walter sat down in his boss's office, his boss poured them each a glass of Jack Daniels Gentleman Jack. He told Walter that he once told himself he would not have a drink before ten in the morning unless he got fired or received a promotion.

"Neither has happened yet, but I'd say we are both damn close to promotions after this news."

His boss told him the contracts were signed late in the afternoon on Thursday, and news broke that same evening. Walter was on an extended weekend trip in Philadelphia and had not seen any emails since walking out of the office early that Thursday afternoon. His boss then told him that the three recent signings were the biggest contracts the firm had seen to date, and that this was exactly what was needed to throw his name into discussions to become partner. An ecstatic Walter told his boss that he had a great team around him and all of their efforts had made it very easy to work with the clients.

"I absolutely agree and think you have built yourself a winning team."

As he left his boss's office, Walter decided to pass by his colleague's desk to chat with her about their recent accomplishment. As he approached, he saw his colleague Malia already speaking with another female employee at the agency, so instead, he signaled for her to stop by his office when she wrapped up her conversation.

Malia was also his mentee, and worked directly on Walter's client markets team.

When he arrived at his office, Walter reviewed his emails and saw an email from the CEO of the company, Ellen Hubert, from Friday afternoon. The email was sent to the entire agency praising them for their efforts last year and highlighting their goals and focuses of this year.

The next email he saw shocked Walter so much that he screamed his joy. A forwarded email of the mass email was sent from Ellen Hubert directly to him. In it, Ellen thanked Walter for helping make 2015 one of the agency's biggest years and congratulated him on his recent success with the contract signings. She declared he was an asset to the agency and ended the email by saying that Walter had a bright future ahead of him, and that she looked forward to his continued success.

Walter was so excited by the email that he reread it and pinched himself on the arm to ensure it wasn't a dream. After reading it a second time, Walter forwarded the email to his boss and told him to prepare another round of shots because he was coming for the corner office. He was so excited that he couldn't wait to tell all of his team, closest friends and family.

As Walter went to close his office door, he pulled out his phone and began to dial a number. While waiting for the person on the other line to pick up, Walter paced around his office in anticipation. After about thirty seconds of ringing, Walter was directed to voicemail. "Hey Bro," he said into the phone, "just got some great news about work. My team and I signed some big contracts recently and when I walked in today, I saw I had an email from our CEO personally thanking me for the work we did last year. Everything we used to talk about as kids is coming true. I will give you more details when you call me back. Love you, kid."

Walter smiled as he hung up the phone.

Malia came to his office to have their discussion but before she could enter, Walter stuck up his index finger, signaling her to wait outside. When he wrapped up his voicemail, Walter waved for her to come in. "Did you see the email from Ellen? How awesome is that? I wasn't expecting it, but I was really happy to get it and I want you and the team to know how proud I am and how much I appreciate you all. I just tried to call my mentor, but he didn't answer. Man, if you would have told me this would be my life today, I would have called you a liar. I was a very different person when I was younger, before my eyes were opened."

Malia looked at him in disbelief. "That's so hard to believe. You're one of the most driven and confident people I know. Since you joined as our leader, I've seen a new strength and vigor with the team. I admire the fact that you are not afraid to make the tough decisions and the team admires the fact that you recognize them for their efforts. It's a nice bonus having a good-looking boss who is also a socialite because your power to network helps us grow as a team."

"Well," Walter scrubbed his face and then shrugged his shoulders. "Before I was a socialite, I was a reclusive loner who preferred to keep to myself. I lost my trust and my confidence. My mentor, who is also my older brother, was the reason I found my confidence and conviction. When we were kids, we were very close until I selfishly turned my back on him. Anyway, I don't want to talk any more about him, I want us to brainstorm ways to celebrate the team for their successful year."

"I have a few ideas, but they won't be cheap. Hopefully Ellen added her credit card number to that email."

Malia gave Walter a rueful smirk, and they both laughed.

CHAPTER 2:

KAROT

The following day, Walter decided to take Malia and a few other members of his team out for a group outing to celebrate their recent accomplishments. Walter knew his team worked hard in the previous year and wanted to award their hard work and loyalty with a team dinner at Medieval Times in New Jersey. He planned to follow dinner up with a night of celebrating at the Lobby nightclub in Elizabeth. As the group's leader, he knew Ellen's thank-you email was appreciated by the group, but he wanted to take it one step further with an outing to show his direct appreciation. Fortunately for him, he convinced the agency to fund this outing.

Unfortunately, Walter's boss was unable to attend, but he told Walter not to spare any expense since it was their way of recognizing the team's hard work.

Since he joined the Karot Agency about two years prior, Walter told himself he was going to learn as much as he could and grow to make partner. Karot was the upper echelon of advertising and since first hearing about it in his sophomore year of college, Walter knew it was a place he wanted to work.

When he finally got in, he told himself he was going to take himself to the next level professionally and the agency to the next level financially. They had been a top advertising agency for many years in a row because of their size and revenue, but Walter knew the thing that kept them at the top was their employee and client satisfaction rate.

When Walter was promoted to associate director with the agency, he knew a large piece of his job was people management. To keep his team motivated, he made it a point to recognize them for their hard work and dedication. Development was also very important to Walter, so he made that a focus of his role, too.

Although the email Ellen Hubert sent the previous week spoke about their remunerative activity of the previous year, to Walter, it spoke to the agency's emphasis on its people. In her message, Ellen joked that outside of the revenue numbers, Karot's success was mostly achieved because of the "late nights and early mornings" of the employees. Ellen had always appreciated the dedication and loyalty of her employees.

Because of the large emphasis on client work, the culture within Karot often called for employees to sacrifice nights and weekends to meet deadlines. This was especially difficult for employees with families. Ellen recognized how hard it was on her employees and began to build a culture around well-being. Since she was promoted from managing partner to CEO, Ellen implemented a comprehensive employee benefits program that allowed any employee who worked before 7 a.m. or after 8 p.m. to expense their transportation. They could also expense their meals during these "off hours." Under Ellen's leadership, Karot also provided each employee with a well-being subsidy they could use toward any mental or physical well-being activity including yoga classes, therapy sessions and gym memberships. Since he regularly began work very early and worked very late, Walter took advantage of this benefit.

Prior to Ellen becoming CEO of Karot, the former CEO was fired because he failed to help the agency recover from an economic downturn. During the downturn, Karot was forced to downsize to ensure it limited the damage from the recession. After the downsizing, the former CEO was caught on tape joking around with other executives about how, despite Karot being the last name of the company's founder, it really stood for "*Kings and Rooks Outlasted Tragedy*." This was a reference to his strategy during the downsizing, which was to fire everyone outside of his executive team plus their seconds or thirds in command. His hope was to rebuild the agency from the top down.

Unfortunately, this strategy failed and their revenue decreased over time. He was fired, and Karot was managed by the Board of Directors for years. Karot did not begin seeing positive gains until Ellen took over as CEO. She began to rebuild the agency from the bottom up and focused on people rather than profits. This strategy helped Karot become the number one advertising agency in the world.

Just this past year, Walter was promoted from his role as senior specialist to associate director, which meant he would serve as project manager and oversee the team. Since the promotion, he told himself he would emulate Ellen's leadership style to manage as a leader instead of as a boss. Keeping his team content was his top priority, and he believed happy employees meant productivity.

As the team pulled up to Medieval Times, they were greeted by the site manager who welcomed them and assured the group that it was in for a special night. Karot handled the marketing and branding for Medieval Times, so both the manager and Walter understood the importance of maintaining this relationship. She escorted the group to the bar first so they could order their first round of drinks. After everyone placed their orders, she escorted them to their tables for dinner and the show. On the way to the table, Walter asked Malia how the group was feeling about the email from Ellen.

"Everyone in the company respects Ellen as a leader because of things like that. The team is pleased, but I am sure they'd prefer to be recognized with extra commas in their paychecks."

The two of them laughed and Walter jokingly told Malia that the day he becomes CEO, he'd ensure that was a top priority. He went on to say, "Ellen's leadership style has had a significant impact on me also. Seeing her commitment to social justice helps reaffirm that she cares about more than just the numbers. I'm also very committed to work in the community, so in a sense, I feel supported by Ellen and Karot. Last year, she was in NYC and we happened to be in the same meeting. I wasn't even sure she remembered me afterward because she didn't say my name once. Just being in the room for me was enough. Getting the email from her showed me that she does know who I am. I'll tell you one thing, if I ever make it to that level, I hope I'm as good as her."

"You're better," Malia beamed at her boss.

After the show, the manager of Medieval Times asked the group what they thought. Everyone said they enjoyed it, and Walter thanked her for the hospitality. On the way to Lobby, Walter sat in the backseat with another member of his team, Robert, and asked him what he thought of Ellen's email.

Robert, who was a tenured employee and much older than Walter, said, "I've never seen anything like it. I've been with the agency for ten years and before Ellen, most emails from the CEO only detailed our numbers and goals. I respect the fact that we're people to her and not just numbers. And I must say, I love the fact that you were promoted to be our lead. Your fresh ideas and perspective helps us succeed. You have a very successful career ahead of you, young man. The team respects you and will continue to give you one-hundred-and-twenty percent every day."

As they pulled up to Lobby, Walter thanked Robert for his feedback and Robert added, "Medieval Times was fun, but I would have been just as happy going to see a movie. With that said, I haven't pulled a night this late in a long, long time."

"Well, I'm sure I can also speak for the group when I say how happy we are that you're here." Walter said, patting Robert on the back as they made their way into the nightclub.

When they arrived to their reserved section, they noticed there were a few bottles of champagne waiting for them on ice. The waitress asked if anyone would like to drink anything besides champagne, and a few members of the team ordered cocktails and beer. When she asked Walter what he'd like to drink, he replied, "Water."

"I hope you're the designated driver. If not, we have to get you a glass of something stronger than water," joked the waitress.

"I'm not driving, but I want to ensure my team is taken care of before I start enjoying myself."

"Wow, that's nice of you. What brings you and your group in tonight?" the waitress asked as she finished writing the drink orders on her notepad.

"We're having a team outing this evening in celebration. We've had a spectacular year, and I want to show my appreciation."

"Wow, I wish my boss was like you." The waitress smiled at Walter and added, "I'm going to grab the other drinks and come back. Hopefully you're ready by then."

As she walked away, Malia told Walter he should get the waitress's phone number because it seemed like she was interested in him. Walter looked at Malia with a smirk on his face and told her he wasn't planning on it, but would decide before the end of the night.

"I'll bet you fifty dollars you can't get her number," said Malia.

"I wouldn't delight in taking your money, but if you double that bet, you've got a deal."

Malia extended her hand. "You're on."

After their drinks arrived, Malia stood up and thanked Walter for organizing the night and bringing the group together. "Let's raise our glasses to our fearless leader who, despite the pressure he faces from the higher-ups, always makes decisions with the team's best interest at heart.

"I'm not sure if you get told this enough, but you're a great boss and we hope you understand how much we appreciate you."

Robert and a few others also reiterated their appreciation for Walter with "here, here" and a few pats on the back, before taking a swig of their drinks.

Walter raised his glass in honor of his team. "Thank you all for what you do, and for making me look good."

For the remainder of the night, the team enjoyed each other's company and the countless number of drinks brought to the table. As his team members slowly began to trickle off, Walter made his way to the main bar to close the tab.

*****

The next day, when Walter arrived to the office, he stopped by his boss's office to tell him how the night went. His boss apologized again for not being able to make it and told Walter he did a great job overseeing the details.

After Walter left his boss's office, he passed by Malia's desk to leave an unsealed envelope for her. She was on the phone, so she smiled and nodded in acknowledgment as Walter headed to his office.

When Malia examined the envelope, she saw the word "invoice" written across the front. Inside, she finds a hand-written bill for one hundred dollars. Malia instantly began laughing hysterically and hung up the phone.

She went into Walter's office, invoice in hand. "I got your message, but I need proof."

Walter merely smirked as he pulled out his phone to show her the text messages from last night and this morning. "Originally, I wasn't planning on asking for it, but when I went to pay our tab, the waitress wrote her number down with a smiley face. Her name is

Brenna and we are planning on seeing each other this weekend."

"I was joking about you getting the phone number, but I must admit, I'm happy to see you were able to pull it off. You're such a great guy, I don't understand why you don't have a girlfriend. You can literally have any girl you want. I've seen girls drool over you."

"I haven't been actively looking because I've been so committed to my work and career. As an African American male, I have to work twice as hard as my counterparts to achieve the same accomplishments. I've got so much more to prove, but I know I can, which is why I work as hard as I do. My job's probably the most important thing in my life right now. I date fairly regularly, but somehow I end up going out with women who fail to impress me. I don't think I have high expectations, I just think I need someone to challenge me to want to stop working as much as I do. Who knows? Maybe Brenna's that person."

CHAPTER 3:

BROKEN MIRRORS

Over the next few days, Walter and Brenna exchanged a few text messages and set up a dinner date for later in the week. He learned that she lived in Elizabeth, New Jersey, with a roommate and worked as a waitress to help pay for graduate school. When Friday arrived, Walter and Brenna agreed to meet at Roma, a restaurant in downtown Jersey City. Walter arrived before Brenna and decided to sit at the bar as he waited.

His phone rang as he waited for his drink. Walter assumed it was Brenna calling to tell him she was running late, but when he looked at his caller ID, he smiled. He picked up the call with a playful, "Finally, the future Denzel Washington decides to call me back. I could've had the Oscar-winning script in my hand and you'd never know."

Walter began to laugh as his brother quickly jabbed back about being sure to remember all the little people. Walter told his brother about the date, which earned him some more brotherly harassment, before moving on to other topics.

Ten minutes later, he saw Brenna walk into Roma and told his brother he'd call him back. He hung up and walked to the front door to greet Brenna with a hug. As they made their way toward their table, Walter took Brenna's coat and hung it on her chair. He then pulled out the chair for her and let her sit before seating himself. Brenna joked how she appreciated him giving her the best seat in the house. Walter sat in his seat and responded, "If you were sitting where I'm sitting and looking at what I see, you'd think differently."

"Stop being such a smooth talker, it's making me blush," Brenna remarked.

"I'm really glad you gave me your number. I was on the fence about whether I was going to ask for it. So, you mentioned you're in graduate school. What are you studying?"

"I originally got my undergraduate degree in sociology from Arizona State, and I moved back home after graduation to pursue my graduate degree in early childhood and family studies. After I finish school, I plan to get a job as a social worker because I want to help families with their overall well-being."

"That sounds like as good as any reason to choose a career," remarked Walter as he stared into Brenna's eyes. "What made you decide to move in that direction professionally?"

"Nothing I can remember, I just saw it as a good opportunity to make money with a stable career. That's it. Unfortunately, I don't have any stories about how I was separated from my family as a child and knew this was my calling or anything like that. Truth be told, I grew up in a pretty nice neighborhood with my entire loving and caring family. Still, I think it's something I'm passionate about. Now, we've done so much talking about me, what about you? What are you passionate about?"

"I haven't really thought about it before, to be honest." Walter shrugged his shoulders in response. "Most of my time has been spent focusing on my career and professional development, which makes me think my passion is in success and technology. I love learning new things about anything digital, and how technology will help us evolve. As a digital associate director for an advertising agency, I have to stay up-to-date with all the innovation and growth in tech companies. I've sort of become obsessive about everything technology related. Outside of that, I can't say I'm passionate about anything else."

He took a sip of his wine and began to think more seriously about Brenna's question. "Like yourself, I'm passionate about the well-being of others. I believe karma is a real thing, and I'm always trying to ensure my good karma outweighs the bad."

As they wrap up dinner, Brenna mentioned that the night was still young and asked if he'd like to continue somewhere else.

"Sure," Walter said. "We can head to see a movie if you'd like. Newport has a great theater that's open late."

Brenna leaned in closer so only Walter could hear. "I'd like that, but I'd be even happier if we could watch a movie back at your place. It would be cheaper and probably more comfortable for us."

"I'd love to have you over, but I've got to warn you, my apartment is a little messy."

"In the few days I've known you, I think I can comfortably say you are probably one of the most well put-together guys I've ever met. If that's any indication, I'm sure your apartment won't be too bad."

Walter handed the waiter his credit card to settle their tab, and they walked out of Roma. The pair got in Brenna's car and drove to Walter's building. After she parked, Walter jumped out of the car first and went around to open Brenna's door. He reached in, taking Brenna's hand to help her out of the car.

As they entered the building, the concierge welcomed him back and told Walter he received a certified letter delivered to his apartment.

"Thank you! How about the Knicks, huh? Why do they continue to break my heart?" asked Walter as he made his way toward the elevators.

When they got to Walter's floor, he noticed that the laundry room was full of people. "I guess I missed the memo about staying in to do laundry tonight," he joked.

When they got inside Walter's apartment, Brenna asked to use the restroom. When she returned, she noticed his apartment is far from untidy. "You made it sound like I was walking into a college dorm room. Even the bathroom was clean, which is rare for a guy who lives by himself."

Walter laughed as the pair headed to the living room to watch a movie Walter selected, *John Wick*.

*****

The following Monday, Walter picked up breakfast and coffee for his team on his way into the office. When he arrived, he sent out an email calling for a 10 a.m. team meeting to discuss a client in Silicon Valley that sent him a proposal for an advertisement they are looking to launch next year.

Once everyone was seated in the conference room, Walter began, "In reviewing the proposal on the train this morning, I see this advertisement has the potential to be huge. The RFP has already been shared and the potential returns from a successful launch and advertisement can give us gains to replicate last year's numbers. I want to make the focus for this year innovation, growth and development. When you do the same thing, you'll end up with the same results. As we progress this year, I'm brainstorming new ways to reinvent ourselves. I'm happy to announce that Robert will be leading this project with me."

The entire group of twelve began cheering. Robert was surprised but happy about the announcement. He had only expressed his interest with Walter the week before, so the announcement came as a complete surprise.

"After the campaign has launched, I'll be taking more of a back seat and allowing Robert to drive for this project," said Walter.

After the team meeting, Walter asked Robert to hang back for a few minutes while the rest of the team left. After the room emptied, Robert extended his hand to Walter and thanked him for the opportunity.

"That was the last thing I thought you were going to announce. I'm grateful for the opportunity."

Walter was very proud to hear Robert say this. "You're a strong component of my team, Robert, and I'd like to engage your experience."

On his way to his office, Walter opened the certified mail he received the night with Brenna and saw it was the bonus check he was waiting for. Taxes wound up taking out a lot more than he thought, but it was still enough to deposit right away. He didn't feel comfortable leaving a check that size out in the open, so he told the team he was stepping out to go to the bank.

On the way there, Walter received a text message from Brenna. She mentioned how much she enjoyed their time together and how much of a gentleman he was. She also wrote that she was in class and work for the remainder of the week but was already counting down the seconds to the weekend.

Walter quickly texted back, telling her he also enjoyed their night and that he is back at work as well. Within seconds, she asked when she'd be able to see him again, but he decided not to respond because he had arrived at the bank. When he looked inside, he saw each teller had a long line in front of them, so he decided to deposit the check directly into the ATM.

As he walked away from the ATM to head back toward his office, Walter thought he saw the old man from the bus stop a few weeks before.

The man turned the corner on the other end of the block. Walter wasn't entirely sure if it was the same man because of the distance, but remembered the beard and those glasses. He still had questions for the old man and began running to catch up. When he reached the end of the block, he looked around and could not see the old man anywhere. He started walking up the sidewalk in hopes of seeing him, but still nothing.

Confused, Walter turned around and began to head back to his office. The old man's words popped into his head again. As he began walking back toward the office, he replied to Brenna by telling her he'd love to meet her again soon for a coffee.

Brenna replied that she would rather come by his house. She jokingly stated that if he wanted, he could send a car to pick her up.

Walter now began to feel odd about where the conversation was going with Brenna because they had only hung out once, so he asked if she'd like to get lunch and go back to her place. She quickly replied they couldn't go to her place but they could go to his, because she was a broke college student and he's wealthy.

Walter realized the red flag that caused him feel weird was the fact that he sensed Brenna had ulterior motives. He continued walking until he reached the end of the block, and told Brenna he couldn't see her again. He added that he enjoyed their time together, but after looking at his schedule for the next few weeks, he just wouldn't have time for her. He ended his message by wishing her good luck with graduate school.

When he arrived back at his office, before he had a chance to ponder the conversation with Brenna or the old man sighting for too long, Walter got an instant message from Malia. She told him he made the right decision appointing Robert as project lead for this new engagement. She added that Robert had always performed at a higher level than a coordinator, but because their previous leader was more focused on his own professional growth than the team's, he didn't listen to anything the team said.

For a moment, Walter considered telling Malia about the old man from the bus stop, but stopped himself. He told himself that what happened was a random occurrence and probably meant nothing. He decided then to leave that moment in the past.

Instead, he told her about what happened with Brenna and their conversation from that morning. He then thanked her for her input on Robert and told her, "Like I said before, if ten years ago you would have told me this is how my life would be, I'd have called you a liar. It was a different time, and I was a very different person. I lacked confidence and would probably have continued with a person like Brenna because I needed that assurance. I needed to feel like I meant something to someone, so there was a point where I was very sensitive to the things I was attached to. I was very guarded and protective of things. Being able to cut it off with Brenna is something I wouldn't have been able to do before, because I would have forced myself to become the person she thought I was in an effort to secure her companionship. I was hurt once, so I was afraid to be hurt again. One way I prevented myself from being hurt was to attempt to cut out the hurtful person from my life instead of address them head on and learn from the situation."

"You could've fooled me. You seemed like you were the life of the party growing up. I would have pegged you as a socialite."

Walter told her that he may be a socialite now, but back then he was a broken loner who swore off the world until he was disproven by the one person he thought he lost.

PART II
MY BROTHER'S KEEPER

CHAPTER 4:

I WILL ALWAYS PROTECT YOU

Walter - Middle School - **Fifteen Years Ago**

The first period bell rang and the teacher signaled for the students to be seated. The math teacher, Mrs. Gale, announced that the day's class would be about exponents. The class collectively responded with a disappointing "sigh" that made the teacher giggle.

"I know math isn't the most popular subject," she told them, "but if you ever expect to be able to count your paychecks one day, you will need to know the fundamentals."

A hand instantly shot in the air and a young girl stood up with her question. "Mrs. Gale, my mother says if I get good grades and go to a good college, I can pay someone to do my paycheck for me. Is that true?"

Mrs. Gale laughed again and told the student her mother probably meant she could pay someone to do her *taxes*. "Sadly, Uncle Sam regulates paychecks for us and he makes sure he gets his cut."

The same girl then asked, "Did Uncle Sam take your class and have to do exponents?

The entire classroom erupted in laughter and even Mrs. Gale got a chuckle out of the question.

The students started chattering and Mrs. Gale told the class to settle down so she could take attendance.

She began to announce student names, looking up after each one for confirmation that they were actually in class.

"Ralph Abbott? Lucie Bain? Walter Benine?"

After she finished with the last name on her roster, she told the students to pull out their textbooks and turn to page seven.

As she began to write on the board, another teacher came into the room and whispered something in Mrs. Gale's ear. Mrs. Gale's normally cheerful face instantly turned into a look of shock and horror. She told the class to read page seven and answer the questions on page eight, and that she would be right back.

She left the room with the other teacher and the students sat at their desks, confused. They began to talk amongst themselves instead of doing the requested reading and equations. Most students got up from their seats to move freely around the room and talk in their groups, all except Walter Benine, who remained in the third seat of the first row. Instead of socializing, Walter was doing the reading with his head down to focus. As he prepared to move on to the questions on page eight, Mrs. Gale returned to the class in tears and said she had some very serious news.

"Reports are coming in stating there was a terrorist attack in Manhattan this morning. Details are still very uncertain, but the reporters are saying there was a plane crash. Are there any students in here who have cell phones? For those of you who do, I want you to contact your parents and let them know you are okay. For those of you who do not have cell phones, please form two single lines on each end of the classroom. The line along the wall closest to the front door will use my cell phone to contact your parents. The line along the window to the back wall will use the classroom phone."

Because he was in the third seat, Walter could have been one of the first students in line to use the teacher's phone, but instead he ran out of the class to the other side of the school and into the eighth grade wing. When he arrived at a classroom, he opened the door and walked inside.

His first observation was that the class was running as normal and his walking in had disrupted the curriculum. It seemed as though the class had not been made aware of the attack. He disregarded this fact and walked up to a boy in the first row, asking him if he had heard the news about what happened in Manhattan.

"Justice, is everything okay? Why is your brother here?" asked the teacher.

Walter explained to the teacher and the rest of the class what Mrs. Gale told him about a terrorist attack that occurred that morning.

"You should not joke about things like that, young man. I am not sure what you heard," replied the teacher, "but you will need to leave the class immediately."

Walter reiterated the news and told the teacher he wasn't joking. The teacher saw the distress and confusion on Walter's face and began to think he was telling the truth. She reached out to the principal's office for confirmation and while speaking with the secretary, dropped the classroom phone. When she picked it back up, she told the secretary she was coming to the office.

"I want you all to stay in your seats and review your textbooks. I'm not sure what's going on, but I'm going to get more information." With that, the teacher exited the classroom.

Walter watched as the teacher left the room and turned his attention back to his brother. "Justice, we need to go back to my class. Mrs. Gale is letting students use her cell phone to call their parents, and we need to let Mom and Dad know we are okay."

Justice followed Walter back to Mrs. Gale's class. When they arrived, Mrs. Gale scolded Walter for leaving the room without first notifying her.

"I needed to make sure my brother was okay," said Walter. "I didn't have a chance to ask you because you looked worried, Mrs. Gale. I was also worried about my brother and without thinking I ran out of the class. I'm so sorry. I just had to make sure he was okay."

She smiled, then handed the boys her cell phone. "Call your parents and let them know you're okay."

Justice grabbed the phone and dialed their mother's number. When she didn't pick up, he tried their father instead.

"Hi Dad, Walter and I are okay. The teacher told us what happened in Manhattan and we tried to call Mom, but she didn't pick up."

"Glad you both are okay," their father said with a relieved sigh. "Your mother wasn't feeling well this morning so she decided to stay home instead of commuting into the city for work. Try calling the house phone. Stay there in school. I love you both."

When the boys called the house phone, they connect with their mom. "Boys, stay there. I'm watching the news and I'm getting dressed. Stay in your class with the teacher and I'll be there shortly."

While they waited, Walter and Justice sat in Mrs. Gale's class and watched as other students' parents came to pick them up. The boys saw the fear and sadness in the faces of some of the other parents and began to worry. They didn't fully understand the extent of the incident, but believed it was more serious than they knew. When their mother finally arrived at school, the boys ran out to her minivan and gave her a big hug.

That night, their parents sat down with the boys to help them calm down and discuss what happened that morning in detail.

"Today," their father said slowly, "was a reminder of how scary the world can be. This was an attack meant to destroy this country's strength. One of the most important lessons we can take away from today is the fact that you and your brother were there for each other. There is nothing more important than family. You must always remember that."

Their mother then pulled out two small jewelry boxes and handed one to each of the boys. "Your father and I got these for you a year after Walter was born. We wanted to ensure you had something from us that represented your inner strength as Benine children. After the events of today, we feel now is an appropriate time to give you these gifts that you can keep for the rest of your lives."

The boys opened their boxes to find a necklace with a pendant attached to it. On Walter's necklace, there was a bee pendant with his name and birthdate inscribed on the back. On Justice's necklace, there was a butterfly pendant which also had his name and birthdate inscribed on the back.

"Not to sound ungrateful," started Justice slowly, "but is there any reason I have a butterfly? Was there no other animal that describes me better than a butterfly?"

Their father explained. "Growing up, we saw some of the worst sides come out in people. Before the civil rights movements, African Americans were looked down on and seen as animals. They treated us like second-class citizens and made most minorities feel inferior. One of the people who fought the adversity and rose above it was Mohammed Ali. Before he would enter the ring, he used to say he could 'float like a butterfly and sting like a bee.' This one quote defined his agile approach to challenges and his strength to take or return any punches that were thrown at him. That's why the butterfly. That's why the bee."

The boys smiled and their mother said, "As you boys began growing up, we noticed Justice was becoming agile, very passive, and was maturing very quickly. Like a butterfly, you are beautiful, very social and have never been afraid to spread your wings and branch out. In that same period, we began to see Walter grow as a protector. When you played with your toys, there would always be a hero because you believed there was always someone worth saving. You care so much for others and always puts the needs of others ahead of your own.

"Leaving your class this morning to go check on your brother was a perfect example of this. A male bee does everything in its life for its queen. The way it serves others resemble you and we want you to continue to be that protector." Their mother looked between them. "If you keep your hearts pure and your heads level, these pendants will always represent you."

The boys looked at each other and then at their parents. The love that filled the room was almost tangible. Finally, their mother smiled and said, "I'm going to take the rest of the week off, and I want you boys to stay home with me. Tomorrow, we'll go get you boys cell phones so you can always reach us."

As the brothers went to bed that night, their parents kissed them both and reassured them that they would be okay. On the way out, they turned off the lights and closed the door behind them.

"Are you tired?" Justice asked.

"No, I'm not. I can barely sleep after today," replied Walter.

Because they shared a bedroom, they spent most nights staying awake for hours talking about life, school, video games and friends. That night, they spoke about what happened in school and how lucky it was that their mom stayed home that day.

"I didn't know what was going on, even when Mrs. Gale mentioned it," Walter said. "It wasn't until she returned to class crying that I knew it was serious. Do you think the terrorists are going to attack our school next?"

"No, I don't. I heard they killed themselves during the attack," replied Justice.

There was then a long silence, and Justice heard Walter quietly crying.

"What's wrong?" he asked.

"The terrorists killed all those people for nothing and had it not been for her being sick, they could have killed mom, too. Even though Mom and Dad are old, I want them to live forever. I'm scared they're going to come to school next and kill me."

"Walt," Justice told him, "you are my best friend and I will never let anything happen to you. Like Mom and Dad said, what happened today was an example of how scared people do scary things. The terrorists will never come to the school. Even if they do, they'll have to go through me first. As your older brother, I want you to know that I'll always protect you, no matter what."

Over the next eight months, the boys were inseparable at school and at home. Their parents were good friends with the next-door neighbors, so often times they found themselves at their neighbors' house for milk and cookies. The neighbors were an elderly Hispanic couple who did not have any children, so they enjoyed regular visits from the boys. They used to babysit both when they were younger, and even taught them Spanish.

In the colder months, when the boys were not visiting their neighbor's house, they holed up in their bedroom and played video games. For hours, the two lost themselves in Mario Kart, Super Smash Brothers and Goldeneye.

Any time there were selections for a backyard sports team, Justice was normally chosen first, which made every pick after that a gamble. People wanted to play *with* Justice and never against him. Walter enjoyed sports, but realized more of his interests came from the bonding it allowed him with Justice.

After school one Monday afternoon, Justice came home and told Walter and their parents he had some exciting news. "The coach from the high school freshman football team contacted my gym teacher and told him he wanted me to come out for football tryouts this summer. He also invited to come watch them play a flag football game."

Their parents were excited for the news, but Walter was upset. He didn't tell Justice so, he simply went to their room to sulk. Justice was going to high school the following year and they would not see each other regularly like they do now. That night during their nightly conversation, Walter asked Justice if he could go to high school with him. Justice laughed.

"Once you graduate from middle school in two years, we'll be together in high school," he said.

"Well, you said you'll always protect me. How can you do that from high school?"

"No matter what school we're in, I will always have your back. You just need to remember that."

A few weeks passed and Justice received his invitation to the flag football game at the high school. It was organized by the varsity players and used as a tool for them to see which underclassmen maintained their strength and speed during the offseason.

Justice was not yet an underclassman, so he knew the invitation was special. He wasn't sure what to expect from the game, but figured he could at least go and see what the current team looked like. When he arrived at the field, the coaches saw him in the stands and invited him to lace up and run a few plays. Justice was a little reluctant at first, but decided to participate. During the game, he not only scored multiple touchdowns, but caught an important pass with seconds left that put his team in position for the win. After the game, Justice was approached by the high school coaches, who reiterate their interest in having him attend tryouts.

Justice left wearing a big smile, and as he walked home, he began to think about what the coaches told him. Walter was his best friend, but he was also in middle school, which meant Justice would be alone next year. He told himself that he'd attend the tryouts, which were scheduled for the following weekend, just to see how it went. School was now over and he was ready to make this a great summer.

*****

Following tryouts, Justice felt confident that he did everything he could. He wasn't sure what the coaches thought, but felt he held his own. Less than a week later, he received a call from the coaches to congratulate him on making the junior varsity team. Justice was excited, but knew it was going to be a big challenge for him since he had never played organized ball. He decided to invest time to learn more about the game and what it would be like to play high school football. He spent the final weeks of summer vacation studying plays, practicing catches and running drills.

Unfortunately, Walter had no interest in running drills with his older brother so during that time, he found himself hanging out with Justice less and less.

The team ran three-a-days during the first two weeks of practice, which meant Justice was gone from sunrise to sunset. Walter began to feel animosity toward the football program and blamed them for ruining their last summer together.

One day, after the three-a-day sessions were over, Walter went to their shared bedroom to see if Justice wanted to go to the ice cream parlor. Justice agreed to go and told Walter he'd be ready in a bit. Unfortunately, as he got dressed, Justice remembered there was a team dinner at one of the player's houses so he asked Walter if he could have a rain check for the ice cream.

Walter told himself that this new Justice was always rushing and never had time for him. Walter decided to allow Justice to be the person he had become. He told himself he would avoid Justice from then on, because now his older brother was a jock who had no time for him. He thought it was going to be difficult at first, but realized that being in different schools would make it easier.

*****

Over the days leading up to the end of the summer, Walter only talked to Justice when Justice said something first. There was no hostility on Walter's part, but deep down, he was filled with sadness, disappointment and distrust. He and Justice had spent their entire childhood together and now he was simply left to deal with life alone. Justice assumed Walter was busy with middle school activities while he was invested in football and his upcoming year of high school. For that reason, seeing Walter less and less did not come off as concerning.

Walter finally realized how alone he was on Justice's first day of high school. That entire summer, he knew Justice was going to go to a different school, but he figured they'd spend their last summer together anyway. Because of the commitments Justice made to the football team, plans didn't work out that way. Justice spent most of the summer before freshman year at football practice and team events. To Walter's dismay, he started the first day of school alone.

On that first day, Walter arrived at school earlier than everyone else because he wanted map the route in the hallways he would use daily. Because he was in a new grade, he planned to come in early until he was comfortable with this new area of the school. Since Justice was no longer there to help ease the transition, Walter made it a point to get comfortable on his own.

CHAPTER 5:

TRUST ISSUES

Walter - High School

Two very few short years later, Walter began his freshman year. This new learning environment was something Walter did not think he was ready for. The middle school was smaller. Academically, he was one of the top students in his class, which meant he was in classes with other top students. Because it was a public school, there weren't many kids in the advanced classes, so Walter felt comfortable there.

Coming into a new school was going to be eye opening. Walter knew he would have a larger group of students to try to avoid on a daily basis. Walter was a shy, reclusive, intelligent young man who found himself enjoying the comfort of a good book instead of the company of people. Since Justice had gone to high school two years earlier, Walter found solace in reading and writing. His favorite past time was getting lost in the stories or adventures of brave heroes like Indiana Jones or reading biographies like Paul Robeson's memoir, *Here I Stand.*

Today was his first day, and he feared the next ten months of mornings would be filled with the same intimidation and depression.

That morning, Walter boarded the bus and quickly located the first available seat, in the second row. Most of the other seats were already occupied by one or more students, so he knew he didn't have many options. Despite that fact, after sitting down, Walter wondered if he should have chosen somewhere else to sit. As the bus turned the corner to pull up to the high school, an intimidated Walter slowly got up from his seat and walked toward the back of the bus. His fear caused him to move away from the front exit in an attempt to hide in the back.

He did not feel ready to go into the school and instead wanted to duck down in the back and wait for the bell to ring signaling the end of the day. As he began to take a few steps toward the back of the bus, he heard a male freshman whisper, "What are you doing?"

Walter froze in his tracks.

"I know someone in the back of the bus and I'm going to go sit with them," Walter lied.

"Everyone knows the back of the bus is filled with upperclassmen," the same kid tells him, "so I don't think that would be the best place for you to try and hide."

"Yeah, everyone knows that," adds another kid. "I'm petrified to go to school, but I'm more afraid of the people sitting in the back of the bus."

Walter extended his hand to the first boy. "Well, nice to know I'm not the only one who's scared. I'm Walter Benine."

"Nice to meet you Walter. I am Xavier Oku, but I go by 'X' for short. I was looking forward to the girls in high school, but I think I changed my mind."

The other kid then reached out to shake Walter's hand. "My name is Sheun Thompson and I'm just as scared as the two of you. Even the bus seems bigger in high school."

The bus pulled up to the dropoff spot and the boys departed. As they entered the school, they saw some big differences. The hallways were larger and the students seemed louder. This was a big change after their quiet middle school experiences. Walter assumed the wider hallways were because the students were also so much bigger.

He knew being reclusive had its perks. It had allowed him to become very observant, and he noticed all the changes large and small. His next thought, while looking around, was how most of the girls he knew from middle school had blossomed into women over summer break.

He also noticed that most of the middle school sports stars who were used to receiving all kinds of reverence were now back at the bottom of the totem pole with the other freshmen. The varsity jacket was the new badge of honor and unless you had one, you were no one worth knowing.

As the students made their way toward their first period class, the boys compared schedules and learned they had most of their classes together. This came as a relief to all three, who then began to describe how much different their middle schools were from high school.

"In middle school," Walter said, "no one bothered me and I was able to get in and out. Everyone was small like me, so I didn't have to worry about the pressure from bullies or other students looking down on me."

X agreed. "All the students were worried about in my middle school was playing sports, trying to find a date and kissing girls."

*****

After the first two weeks, Walter, Xavier and Sheun watched as the jocks took advantage of the privileges that came with being able to catch a football or shoot a basketball. Most moved through the halls as if they were untouchable while everyone else watched in adoration. The trio joked about how the jocks ran the school, not the principal or teachers.

The boys laughed in agreement and continued walking through the hallway to class.

"I wish," said X, "I knew a jock, because I want to learn how to talk to the upper-class girls."

Sheun agreed. "I wish I knew a jock, too, because I want people to respect me. Knowing a jock would be a first-class ticket to the top."

Walter nodded his head in agreement but didn't say anything.

One day while walking in the hallway the following week, Walter and his friends saw a group of athletes walking toward them. Walter attempted to turn around, but one of the jocks began to run toward the three boys.

Xavier and Sheun feared they were about to receive their first "Freshman Friday" beatdown and also turned to walk away until a voice called out, "Walter!" The three freshmen froze in their spots. Xavier and Sheun looked at Walter, who had his head down. The other two boys followed suit, silently accepting whatever fate was in store for them.

The athlete who called to him was wearing a varsity jacket with the last name "Benine" across the back. He was now right behind the trio with a few friends in tow. Again he called out Walter's name.

Walter, Sheun and Xavier turned around at the same time.

"Hey guys, I'm Walter's older brother, Justice. I'm a junior at the school, and on behalf of myself and my friends, I want to welcome you," Justice extended his hand to the boys, then looked to his brother. "Hey Walt, I left my lunch money at home. Do you happen to have a few extra dollars?"

"I don't," Walter replied rudely, turning around to walk away.

Xavier and Sheun turned around with him, and began to rush after Walter.

"Please tell me that kid is not really your brother," X asked. "You have a jock for a brother? He's so nice. That just might disprove everything I thought about jocks."

"He may seem friendly, but he only cares about himself," Walter insisted. "I don't care if he's one of the 'cool kids.' I don't want people thinking my family is stupid. Athletes are manipulative assholes who get things done by having others do them for them. I'm sorry I didn't tell you guys. Justice and I actually used to be best friends, but when he started playing sports, I could no longer trust him."

The boys laughed and told Walter that that was the dumbest thing they've ever heard in their lives, but forgive him for not telling them about his brother.

As time passed, Walter and his two friends become more comfortable with their new school. They spent a lot of their time in the library and after about two months of keeping to themselves, they decided to attend their first Friday night football game. The game was also at the end of their first homecoming week. Unbeknownst to the boys, it was the biggest game of the season, which meant most of the school was at the game.

As they made their way to the bleachers, the boys saw how many people were there, and Sheun stopped walking.

"Hey uh…guys, I don't feel so hot. I think I'm going to go home and get some rest."

Walter turned back, noticing his friend was very pale. "It'd be dumb to turn around now. Are you feeling sick as in throw-up, or sick as in scared? If we want to be more than just small, frail freshmen, this may need to be our first step."

"I agree with Walt," said X. "If we can make it through this game, we can make it through any game."

Sheun smiled, admiring his friends' courage. "You guys are right. The school is just so new to us. I think once we become a little more comfortable, we'll probably love it."

The three decided to stop by the concession stand first, and then proceeded to their seats. When they got to the bleachers, Xavier asked Walter if Justice was playing.

"I'm not sure, to be honest. We don't really talk much. Justice tried to start conversations sometimes, but I usually keep my answers short."

Almost immediately, the boys heard the announcer mention that Justice caught the ball and had gained twelve yards. X and Sheun leaned over to high-five Walter in their excitement, but Walter just sat stone-faced in his seat.

Later in the game, the announcer again yelled in excitement when Justice caught a forty-five-yard pass to score another touchdown for the home team. Everyone in the crowd went crazy except Walter, who remained quietly in his seat watching the field.

Xavier yelled over the crowd. "Walt, stop sitting there like a gargoyle and celebrate your brother with us!"

Despite the crowd's cheers, Walter remained unamused. When the excitement died down and the fans were seated again, X asked Walter what his real beef with his brother was. Walter doesn't answer. Someone behind them in the crowd overheard the boys talking and asked if Justice was Walter's brother.

Walter doesn't respond, but his friends confirmed it anyway.

"That's awesome!" the kid behind them gushed. "Justice is the best player this team has had in a long time. A lot of people say he's really nice, too. I personally haven't met him, but I hope I can one day."

Walter thanked the kid and went back to watching the game, but not before Sheun saw a small smile playing at the corners of Walter's mouth. It is in this brief moment that Sheun realized that Walter's stone-cold act toward his brother was not real. He knew deep-down inside that Walter loved and admired his brother.

*****

More than halfway through his first year of high school, Walter and his two friends learned that the African American Studies group is taking a trip to the Inner Harbor in Baltimore, Maryland, in April. The three freshmen talked to each other excitedly about going on the trip. For Xavier and Sheun, the chance to avoid school held real appeal. Walter on the other hand saw it as a chance to get away from Justice and his friends, even if just for a day.

When Walter found out Justice was going on the trip, he considered taking his name off the sign-up sheet until Xavier and Sheun talked him out of it. They also reminded Walter that they had already sat on the sidelines for four months.

"It's time to start working toward our popularity," Xavier stated.

They joked that Walter would be a fool to miss the trips simply because he was afraid of a few jocks. Walter realized that despite knowing his friends are joking, he also knew they are right. From their small town in New Jersey, it was a three-hour trip and there are just more than a hundred people going. He thought to himself, *what are the chances of seeing Justice?* Walter didn't share anything with his friends, but he was secretly hoping his brother would be on one of the *other* three buses.

If Justice was on another bus, Walter thought, the other athletes would follow him and Walter wouldn't have to worry about seeing any of them. He decided to keep his name on the sign-up sheet.

CHAPTER 6:

THE MOMENTS WE KNEW

Walter - Baltimore, Maryland

The morning of the African American Studies group trip, the teachers and students arrived in the school gym for attendance and began to make their way to their assigned bus. After previously speaking with the organizer, Walter learned which bus the athletes were taking, and that he and his friends were on another bus. The organizer did not question the request and happily obliged.

Before leaving the school, the students were assigned to chaperones so each student knew who to report to when they arrived. Fortunately for the boys, Walter, Sheun and X were able to get the same chaperone. Once they arrived in Baltimore, the students met for a group breakfast and an itinerary breakdown of their day.

After breakfast, the group was shown a welcome film that detailed the history of the harbor and how it became a pillar of trade in the 18th century. Most of the students at the school had never traveled to Baltimore before, so the film kept their attention.

After the film, the organizers spoke to the larger group about how important it was for the students to stay with their chaperones and to remain within the harbor area. They made it clear to chaperones and students that under no circumstance should they venture out into the city.

"There's lots to see here, but we don't need anyone getting lost during the first year we hold this trip. If successful, this could potentially become an annual thing."

Just after lunch, the three boys found themselves on the steps of the mall. Their chaperone told them they could stay on the steps of the mall, but should not move an inch until he returned from finding another one of the students who had wondered off into the mall. The boys agreed, deciding to sit on the top of the steps so they could watch boats pass by on the harbor.

The weather was nice, the seagulls were flying and other tourists were out in bunches. The boys talked about how well the trip was going and what their plans were for the remainder of the afternoon.

Walter was happy to be there despite his original reluctance to join. "I haven't seen Justice and his friends once. If I had stayed home, I would've just been twiddling my fingers."

"You're a scared fool," Sheun joked. "I'd kill to have an older brother like Justice. He's kind, popular and handsome. Girls love him, which means they love anyone around him. I'd consider giving up a non-essential body part to join his inner circle."

Xavier slapped his friend on the shoulder. "As a single child, I became a loner because I didn't have someone there with me. I wish I had a brother like yours."

"You guys are right," Walter admitted. "Justice and I had such a great relationship once. We were best friends who did everything together. I didn't care for sports like he did, so we began to become distant. He told me we would be best friends forever, but then left me behind. I went into my shell after that, and I blame Justice for the damaged relationship. I knew it was inevitable that he'd leave middle school, but I didn't think he'd become so involved with sports."

As the boys sat talking and taking in the view, Walter noticed a tough-looking teenage girl approaching Sheun, who had moved towards the bottom of the steps. It looked like she was with another teenage boy, but Walter wasn't sure because the boy was a few steps behind her. The girl then walked up to X and began talking to him.

Walter couldn't hear what they were saying at first, but then heard the girl telling X and his friends to empty their pockets. A stunned Walter couldn't believe they were being robbed in the middle of the day on the Baltimore Harbor mall steps. There were more teenagers around now, and Walter realized the gang had strategically surrounded the boys, catching them one by one.

Where the hell is our chaperone? Walter thought to himself as he looked around. As he watched X hand the girl his watch, wallet and gold necklace just like Sheun had, he knew he was the next target. Walter watched as his friends handed their possessions to the female without any resistance. As the girl made her way to Walter, he briefly thought about his mom telling him that he was the protector. He thought about this responsibility and realized he hadn't protected his friends. He quickly made up his mind to protect what he had left. The girl walked up to Walter and demanded that he "run his pockets."

Without thinking twice, Walter stared her down and told her no.

"Oh, this is the tough guy of the group!" badgered the female thug. She then looked at the others in her group and laughed. When she looked back at Walter, she reached in to grab Walter's pocket, but he knocked her hand away.

"I'm not giving you anything!" Walter said as his voice cracked in fear. Just then, the male directly behind the female stepped in front of Walter and stared him down. As Walter and the male thug stared each other down, Walter clenched his fist in anticipation of the fight he believed he was about to get into. The female thug laughed in frustration at Walter's resistance, and told the male to snatch Walter's gold chain off his neck. When the male attempted to reach in, however, Walter unclenched both fists and shoved the male away, causing him to fall back on a few steps. The male rushed back up the steps in an attempt to frighten Walter, but when he got back in front of him, he stopped and just continued to stare him down.

In that moment, another one of the thugs slipped behind Walter and pulled out a gun, putting it to the back of Walter's head and arrogantly asking him if he was ready to meet his god.

Walter couldn't remember ever being so terrified, and his hands began to tremble. Once Walter felt the gun against his head, he began to think how foolish it was to stand his ground and push the thug backward, but made up his mind to continue standing his ground. He had never seen a gun up close before, let alone had one pointed at him, but told himself that he was committed to his decision to stand up. He doesn't respond to the comment, and instead, closed his eyes. He didn't know whether it was out of fear or bravery, but he *did* know he was not parting ways with the gold necklace his parents gave him.

In that moment, thousands of thoughts run through his mind. He wondered if he had made the right decision to not give away his possessions, and felt a deep regret for not continuing his relationship with Justice. He knew his brother had an immense amount of love for him, but his pride and ego had prevented him from being receptive to it. He told himself then that if he made it through this moment, he would make a better effort to get to know his brother and be better at life.

He also had no intentions of surrendering his possessions to a bunch of thugs who were kids like him. His parents didn't have much and what little they had, they gave to their sons. He also knew it wasn't the smartest decision, but he knew it was the one he made.

After what felt like an eternity with his eyes closed, Walter opened them to see the female thug tap the thug holding the gun. She told him they were leaving, and claimed loudly that Walter was not worth any more of their time. As Walter looked around, he also noticed others in the area had stopped to watch the scene unfold. The thieves preferred to rob with discretion and since they had attracted attention, it was time to leave. Walter figured this would be the best time for him and his friends to leave, so he signaled X and Sheun. The thug who stared Walter down was still directly in front of him, so Walter took one step back and calmly began walking away with his friends.

As the three students left the steps, a million new thoughts ran through Walter's mind. He didn't know whether to call a chaperone, his parents or the police. He had never been robbed before, so he didn't know if he should reach out for help, or keep quiet for fear of retaliation. He decided almost immediately that he didn't fear the retaliation, and that it was best to notify someone.

Justice wasn't the first people who came to mind, but something in Walter told him to call him anyway. As he explained the robbery to his older brother, his voice began to shake due to the shock that suddenly hit him all at once. Quickly telling the story helped Walter realize how real it was. Without hesitation, Justice told Walter to wait where he was, because he was on the way.

Almost immediately, Justice and about eight of his friends arrived at Walter's location. Walter, who was still in a bit of shock, quickly told Justice and his friends what happened as about ten other jocks arrived. Walter saw Justice and his friends becoming upset with the story and finished by pointing in the direction the thieves were walking. Justice looked at his friends and saw that there are were now close to twenty students with him. Among these students are fifteen athletes.

"My younger brother and his friends were robbed by some thugs, and I'm going after them," Justice said. "They probably assumed my little brother was alone and no one is here to protect them. I plan on reminding them that he is *never* alone. I don't expect any of you to join me if you don't want to. I've already ditched my chaperone – as most of you have – so chances are I'll be breaking a few more rules and I don't want anyone else to risk getting into trouble."

The entire group almost immediately announced its commitment to help Justice. "If your brother was robbed, that means one of our brothers was robbed," said one of the students.

The group began to move in the direction of the gang of thieves. They didn't have any particular plan but know they would act when they saw the perpetrators.

In hearing the support he received from Justice and his friends, Walter's shock turned to anger. He decided to join his brother's pursuit of the thieves. When the thieves looked back and saw Justice and his friends running toward them, they scattered in various directions. The thieves weren't sure who was chasing them, but they knew they didn't want to get caught.

Walter, Justice and the rest of their friends run through the city of Baltimore in pursuit of the assailants, chasing the thieves through train stations, residential buildings and a parking garage. For the next fifteen minutes, the boys ran into local shops, a grocery store, a hotel lobby and a farmers' market in hopes of finding the preparators. When they arrived at one of the shops at the farmers' market, one of Justice's friends, Lobas, said he thought he saw one of the thugs up ahead. The boys sprinted forward to grab the person in question from behind, but Walter stared at him in confusion, not recognizing the teen boy and unsure whether he was part of the robbery. Lobas asked the boy where he was twenty minutes prior, but the boy demanded they release him and stated he was at the market. Walter saw the fear in the boy's face and realized the boy was just as afraid of Justice and his friends as Walter was of the thugs. Walter told Lobas and the others that the teen was not involved. Lobas doubted Walter's statement and questioned his decision, but Justice demanded he lets the boy go.

"If my brother said he wasn't involved, he wasn't involved." Justice stated. "The actual thugs are around here somewhere. We just need to find them."

The boys proceeded to the exit of the market, which was located beside another parking garage. Justice thought he saw two of the thieves run into the lower level of a garage, and followed behind. When Walter caught up to Justice, he saw Justice and his friends holding the two kids as a few of the other jocks punched the thieves in the face. Justice asked Walter if these kids were a part of the robbery and Walter confirmed as much.

Walter saw one of the two kids was the male who stood in front of Walter in an attempt to intimidate him. Walter confirmed this with Justice and told him that that was the boy who tried to steal the chain their parents got them. Justice punched both gang members in the face, and the rest of the group joined in the beating. As blood began to run down the mouths of both thieves, Walter saw what was happening and told Justice and his friends to stop. He realized that in that moment, they were no better than the thugs were when they robbed him and his friends. He prompted the group to leave the thieves and exit the garage, which they agreed to do. Before leaving, Lobas told the thieves that they messed with the wrong brother, and their group made its way to the exit.

Afterward Walter, Xavier, Sheun and the group returned to the harbor. As the group made its way back to the group of concerned chaperones who were standing at the harbor with the police, Walter looked at his brother and for the first time in a long time, he was reminded of how much Justice means to him. Walter had been closed off to his brother for most of the past three years, but never once did Justice stop trying to reconnect with him. In one of his most vulnerable moments in life, Walter saw that Justice was quick to step in and protect him. He remembered what it was like when they used to speak regularly, and realized the pure intentions Justice has always had for him.

After they finished giving their accounts of the robbery to the officers and chaperones, Justice asked Walter to take a walk so they can get away from the madness and clear their minds before boarding the bus. Walter seemed fine, but Justice wanted to check to make sure his younger brother really was okay after the ordeal. When Justice asked his brother how he was doing, Walter broke down in tears.

"I almost didn't call you, because I didn't think I could. I hate the person I've become, and I'm so sorry for the way I've treated you over the past few years. I blamed you for leaving me alone, even after you told me you would always be there to protect me. I now know you didn't leave me to leave, you just grew up and pursued different interests."

Justice smiled. "Sure, I've got some new hobbies, but I've never forgotten how important you are to me, Walt. We've been through so much together. You mean the world to me, and like I told you the night of the terrorist attack in Manhattan, I'll always be there for you. I am glad you finally opened up to me so we can get through this."

As the brothers continued their talk, Xavier and Sheun came up to thank Justice for his help. Justice didn't know the boys well, but he knew they were friends with Walter, and he was glad his brother wasn't alone.

"I'll let you catch up with your friends, but hurry back, 'cause the bus will be headed home soon," Justice said.

As the two brothers embraced, Justice whispered something in Walter's ear that made him break down again. X and Sheun didn't hear what was said, but they know it was enough to make the kid who stood his ground in an armed robbery break down and cry.

When the boys got home, their parents allowed them to stay home that Friday because of the ordeal. The boys took advantage of their day off and spent the entire day together.

*****

When they returned to school the following Monday morning, word had gotten out about the robbery and how Walter stood his ground. Some saw his actions as stupid, others believed he was brave. In the following days, Walter found himself amid conversations with people about what happened in Baltimore. He didn't know most of the people he spoke with, but Justice was with him for many of the conversations so his confidence grew. More and more people were learning that Walter and Justice were brothers, and Walter began to become more comfortable meeting new people.

He didn't want any praise or acclaim for not allowing himself to be robbed, but was happy that it opened this line of communication between him and Justice. The incident had also allowed him to meet so many other students that he probably wouldn't have met otherwise. In one of his conversations with Justice, Walter told him that he wanted to be like him.

"I want to have twenty friends who'll run through Baltimore with me out of support. I came into this high school as a timid loner eight months ago, but I think I'm ready to branch out and start meeting more people. Sheun and X are great friends, and they want to meet more people, too. They tell me all the time how much they want to be like you."

"I'm happy to hear you say that," Justice replied, "because meeting people is something I'm very good at. I'd love to help."

Over the remaining months of the school year, Walter and Justice once again became an inseparable pair who did everything together. Justice began working with Walter on everything related to sports, a social life and girls, while Walter showed his brother how to finally hit that 4.0 GPA and helped him refine his already strong Spanish. Through this, the brothers realized just how much they had to offer each other.

One day, as Walter and Justice talked, Walter said,

"Over time, I've watched how articulate you are in conversations, especially with girls. Can you teach me how to do that? My confidence is rising, but I want to get so comfortable in my skin that I can walk up and talk to anyone."

"Well Walt, the secret to these high school girls is making them believe you don't need them. I am a popular athlete and I get good grades; what do I need with one of these girls? With that state of mind, I never lose sight of what's important. It makes it easier to talk to girls, when I can take them or leave them. That's only half the battle. Once you've found one worth talking to, ensure she's the right one. As you start to build relationships, you'll see that you'll encounter a lot of people who see you for who you are, and others who see you for who they believe you are. The group who sees you for who they believe you are will always have other intentions. Some good, some bad. Just be on the lookout, 'cause most of the time, their intentions aren't in your best interest."

Walter took notes, and planned to adopt this method in his life.

Walter was happy with how the year had taken such a positive turn, and he was especially proud of the fact that he was able to become more comfortable with the one group he detested the most, the athletes.

Being around the older kids also equipped Walter with certain communication skills that he could use later in life. He quickly learned to speak their vernacular, which made them more comfortable around him. By the end of the school year, he was speaking with their acronyms and using their slang.

They loved it because they felt Walter was a miniature version of one of the school's most popular students. Justice was also happy with how his friends received Walter. He knew everyone at the school, and his goal was to ensure his brother did, too.

At the conclusion of that school year, Walter officially had his own identify. Although he was known by most as Justice's younger brother, he was seen as a leader of his freshman class. Other students began making active efforts to get to know him, which boosted Walter's confidence. As his popularity grew, so did the interest he received from girls. By the end of his freshman year, he was one of the school's most well-known students.

The events of what happened in Baltimore helped open a door Walter thought was closed forever. The shy kid who walked in ten months ago was gone, leaving behind a suave, confident intellect.

*****

The summer after freshman year, Justice works with Walter on his athletics, music, and fashion. Sports are their bonding topic and Walter is committed to continuing their positive relationship.

By his sophomore year of high school, Walter attends basketball tryouts and ends up making the varsity team. For the remainder of their time in high school, Walter and Justice lead the school in both academics and athletics.

Walter also achieves significant accomplishments in high school. He leads the basketball team to the conference finals and is the division's leading point scorer in his junior and senior years. He graduates with a 4.0 GPA and is the student speaker at his high school graduation.

PART III
HOMECOMING

CHAPTER 7:

THINGS WE FIGHT FOR

Walter – Present Day

So far, the year had been a great one for Walter Benine. Thinking back on the past eleven months, Walter smiled as he thought about the fact that he had already signed three clients to his firm, received a very generous bonus, led a successful fundraising project that generated more than $20,000 for the United Way NYC and was unanimously voted Vice Chairman of their Board of Directors. He knew he was a workhorse who loved achieving success in anything he is a part of. Being able to work in a field he loved made it easy to succeed because he did not see it as work. He viewed his job as him doing what he loved in an industry he admired. It also gave him the flexibility to commit to various volunteer activities, which was important to him.

Walter remembered when, after graduating high school eight years prior, he played two years of college basketball for his university. His first year was still an adjustment period but by the second year, Walter realized he could not perform at as high a level as the others on the team. His high school success was rewarding, but the demand and commitment required at the collegiate level was too much for him to stick with for four years of school. As disappointing as it was, Walter saw it as one of the best decisions he made. His failure as a college basketball player was the determining factor of moving into a field he enjoyed. He realized he was more interested in digital marketing.

While in school, he also joined various social groups at school. He learned the ins and outs of technology while ensuring he remained committed to the community. After what happened in Baltimore, he told himself that he wanted to work with kids to help raise confidence, reduce bullying and foster strong communities for children to grow up in.

It's these commitments that later translate into his career.

Now in his professional career, Walter prided himself on being able to "speak the language of his clients." Most clients who Walter works with are younger and seek representation from businesses that understand them and their culture. Fortunately for the agency and for Walter, he not only spoke the digital language of the millennials, but he was also fluent in English, Spanish, German and American Sign Language. This made him very attractive to all types of clients.

When building relationships, Walter always made it a point to reference his volunteer work. This was a significant commitment in his life and he felt a calling to speak on its value. In an effort to not seem like he was bragging, Walter never spoke about the roles he played with each organization. He usually did not tell people he was a vice chair, or that he was the creator of the coalition unless prompted to do so. He normally just mentioned that it was an important commitment in his life, and that he always made sure to find time to volunteer. Clients loved this about him and often found themselves calling Walter to socialize outside of normal work duties.

Although he preferred to keep his work and personal life separate, he didn't mind when clients became friends. Some of the closest people in his life were once his clients. His ability to create genuine relations even helped him connect with industry leaders he never interacted with.

Once in a web conference with various leaders in the digital advertising world, one of the presidents from another agency characterized Walter as energetic, outgoing and the most resolute person he knew.

He went on to say, "Walter is the most cerebral consultant in the industry, and I hope Ellen is paying him well to keep him happy. There are at least a dozen other agencies ready to pay him for his talents."

This type of feedback was regularly shared about Walter because he had always welcomed new challenges, was never afraid to put his reputation on the line for something he believed in, and thrived on innovation. Despite his position with the agency, competitors viewed Walter as an asset to the industry.

Understanding his value also helped him do his best work and kept him loyal to his current company. He loved his team and was happy to see his efforts recognized. The bonus he received from the three contract signings was allocated toward savings, investments and life insurance. Although he didn't have children, Walter knew he has a brother who he wants to ensure is protected in case he met his maker early.

After allocating his bonus accordingly, the remainder was spent on living the good life. He knew he was young, successful and hungry, so his reward for the success had to be appropriate and extreme. When he was not out with clients or coworkers, he was found wining and dining many of NYC's single women. Walter never went out actively seeking women, but he somehow often found himself in situations to receive many phone numbers.

Much like Brenna, none of the women behind the numbers had panned out to be anything more than someone seeking stability. Most of them saw Walter's lifestyle and assumed they could use him to take care of them. Fortunately for Walter, he always thought back to the advice Justice gave him about paying close attention to intentions

Despite those facts, Walter had enjoyed the exercise of dating since high school. Whether it was something small like going to see a movie with a woman or something a bit more grand like a seven-course dinner at Inakaya, he loved crafting the experience and seeing it through execution.

The restaurants he was known to take dates to typically had extensive wine lists and limited table reservations. Somehow, he always knew someone at the restaurant who greeted him and his date at the door and personally escorted them to a table. The smile that always followed from his date gave him an immense amount of joy. Even if they didn't end up sleeping together, the small bit of narcissist in him still loved to see that smile. These little details had caused women from all over to want more from Walter.

The women he dated were one thing, but he found that his closest relationships remained with the people from his childhood. Specifically, the people who knew him before he became the Walter Benine most knew today. Sheun and X were the only two friends who had been with him through it all.

After high school, the three boys went to different universities but maintained their friendship and communicated regularly through group chat and video messaging. Sheun went to community college for two years, then to Penn State, where he received a degree in social sciences with a minor in civil engineering. He then joined AmeriCorps and moved to Peru to work as a farmer and teacher for sixteen months. He settled in Philadelphia upon his return.

Xavier went to Howard University and received his degree in biomedical science. Not long after graduating from Howard, X married his college sweetheart and they moved to Washington D.C. Walter and Sheun were groomsmen in his wedding, and helped him move to DC.

Both relationships are very important to Walter, but the most important relationship to Walter was the one he had with his brother. Justice was happy with the man Walter has become, and even happier to hear about his professional success.

*****

When December rolled around, Walter thought back on the year he'd had and smiled. So many accomplishments to be proud of, but none compared to the fact that Justice was moving back to the East Coast at the end of the week. For the past five years, Justice had lived in Los Angeles and pursued a career in acting. After graduating high school, Justice went to USC where he met people in film and television. After graduating, he secured a role on a show and had been in LA ever since. His coming home was due to the fact that he recently signed on with an upcoming Netflix drama that would be filmed in New York City. Prior to that, the brothers had only seen each other during holidays and sporadic visits throughout the year.

This was the first time they'd be living in the same place since high school. Justice knew he was coming back in a good period of his life. Like Walter, he had no children, and had just broken up with his longtime girlfriend. Outside of rent and friends, Justice had no significant obligations in LA to prevent him from moving home. He, too, had dated many women, dined at many delicious restaurants and was living a wonderful life on the West Coast. But, he knew he was missing the one constant he had in his life, his family. He also missed the season changes he was used to on the East Coast. The LA sun was nice, but the absence of snow made winters seem lackluster.

The brothers regularly spoke on the phone and Facetimed when they were free. Because Walter traveled often for work, they sometimes coordinated schedules to allow themselves to take advantage of new cities on the company's dime. It wasn't very often, but the times they could arrange for this ensured they enjoyed themselves. Seeing Justice happy was something Walter can't get enough of. The times Justice was able to visit NYC, Walter made it a point to give him something exciting to talk about when he returned to L.A.

*****

During one particular visit back in 2014, Walter told Justice that he would send a car to pick him up from the airport. When Justice arrived at Newark Liberty Airport that Friday evening, he called Walter to find out where the car was.

Justice was confused because the only cars waiting were three Ubers, which had people in them already, and a bunch of yellow cabs. Past that, the only other vehicle around was a bus.

The bus door opened and he heard Jay Z's "Empire State of Mind" playing. Walter emerged from the bus with a bottle of champagne and two champagne flutes.

"Oh gosh, how much did you spend on this nonsense?" Justice laughed.

"I didn't spend a dime. I was able to convince Karot to sponsor this party bus as 'entertainment' because it was being used as a client entertainment item. I've got a strong relationship with my clients, so when I have favors, they generally agree to participate."

When Justice got on the bus, he hugged Walter and told him to "watch how the OG takes care of business." They partied in the bus for the next three hours, driving around Manhattan until they pulled up to a loft on the Upper East Side.

When Justice flew back to the West Coast on Monday morning, he had only had six hours of sleep, was $6,000 richer after an impromptu visit to Atlantic City and had a slew of new numbers in his phone. The boys loved when they caught up, and often laughed about these nights.

*****

Justice moving home meant Walter had to arrange for a night that produced a memorable story even bigger than the one about the party bus. He was determined to make his brother's welcome home extravagant and did not see any particular limitations on why he couldn't do just that.

Through his regular patronage at many of NYC's most exclusive restaurants and nightclubs, Walter knew nothing was off limits. If needed, he was ready to call in major favors to make Justice's return memorable.

Conveniently, Justice was returning just before New Year's, which meant Walter could kill two birds with one stone. He could throw a killer New Year's Eve party and also have it serve as a welcome home party for Justice. He planned to invite X, Sheun, some colleagues, a few clients and a bunch of other mutual friends he and Justice had. Many of the friends Justice and Walter had from high school still lived around North Jersey and maintained contact with the brothers through Facebook.

Walter also had plans for Justice to live with him until he was able to get his own place. He had a two-bedroom condo in downtown Jersey City and figured it would be perfect for Justice, who would also be working in Manhattan.

Despite all the great things that had happened throughout the year, Walter still couldn't stop thinking about the old man from the bus stop. Every time he thought about his success in 2016, his mind eventually drifted to that conversation. He wasn't sure what made him turn around that day, but told himself that whatever it was, it opened a dialogue between him and the old man that he felt ended unceremoniously. There were so many questions he had, but no way to have them answered. He began to ask himself if the moment was even real.

Unfortunately after the occurrence, something told him not to tell Malia so there was no one he can confirm the occurrence with. Walter now felt he was wasting time thinking about it and began to convince himself that the meeting with the old man was either a dream or one of those rare occurrences that happen in life but nothing comes from it. He resolved to stop thinking about the situation and move on with life as if it never happened.

CHAPTER 8:

THE HILLS HAVE EYES

Justice- December 2016

On the morning of Monday, December 19, Justice was awakened by someone tapping his shoulder. When he opened his eyes, he saw a half-naked woman who he did not know. She was complaining about the noise outside. Justice took a moment to wipe his eyes then looked at the woman again. He vaguely remembered meeting her last night at the going away party his friends hosted for him.

Tomorrow will be his last day in Los Angeles before he leaves for New York City, and his friends decided to throw him a surprise dinner last night at Rustic Canyon. The party had a lot of the actors and actresses who worked with Justice over the years, as well as many of his other friends from his social life.

As an actor in Hollywood, he had made a lot of friends in LA, but Justice was pleasantly surprised to see so many new faces at his dinner. As he thought back, he remembered being introduced to the woman who was in his bed, by one of his actress friends right before being handed a round of shots. Now, the woman was glaring at him. Justice asked her what was wrong.

With an exhausted look she replied, "There is a lot of noise coming from outside of your apartment. It woke me up."

Justice looked at his clock. It was 8:12 a.m. "The kids are on their Christmas vacation, so they normally start their day early. They're just having fun and staying out of trouble."

"Well, it woke me up," she grumbled.

Justice laughed and jokingly replied, "Well, I guess I got my money's worth, because I pay them to be my alarm clock."

Unamused, the woman threatened to leave if Justice did not do something about the noise. Unbeknownst to her, Justice doesn't remember her name and was actually hoping that she will leave.

When he did nothing but lay back on his pillow she saw it as her sign and began getting dressed. As she searched for her clothes, she told Justice she had a fantastic night and asked him if he was surprised by the dinner.

"No," he sighed. "Unfortunately, my friend Samantha spilled the beans when she tried to coordinate with me. Since I was only in L.A. for a few more days, Samantha wanted to confirm I hadn't made any other plans."

While his unknown friend got dressed, Justice offered to call her an Uber, which arrived less than ten minutes later. When the car pulled up, he walked her downstairs and opened the car door for her.

"I had a great time. Sorry again about the noise this morning," he gave her a hug and a kiss before the woman got into the car.

After getting into her seat, the woman told Justice she'll call him. Since Justice still doesn't remember her name, he told her to text him instead because his phone service is spotty. She agreed, and closed the car door.

The young kids stopped playing basketball to watch the scene until the Uber driver pulled away from the curb. When the car was gone, one of the boys threw the ball to Justice and asked him to play a round of horse with them. Since Justice was the reigning HORSE champion for this basketball court, he happily accepted. While shooting with the kids, he joked that he will be leaving for New York tomorrow and unless they beat him today, his name will be memorialized forever.

"Why are you leaving? Seems like you only just got here," one of the boys asked.

Justice drained an easy outside shot. "I just signed on to play the main character in this new Netflix show that's being filmed in Manhattan. I have to sacrifice if I ever want to win an Oscar. I also want to show you guys how attainable success like this is."

"I'd rather be a basketball player like LeBron James one day," said another boy, puffing out his chest. I want to have a big house, nice car and all the girls."

"You don't need all that stuff, other than a good woman, to be happy. You need to be able to speak well, dress well and go after anything you want. That's what the game-changer is. People like LeBron knew this formula and pursued and achieved it.

"Women and life are like a game of chess," Justice went on to explain. "Understanding your end goal and thinking three steps ahead will help you get there. It doesn't matter if you're a basketball player, an accountant or a fast food worker. If you got it, you got it, and if you don't, there's nothing you can do about it."

The boys laughed and asked Justice if he's got it. Justice laughed too, and took one step back. He gripped the basketball with both hands, bent his knees jumped and released the ball. As the ball soared through the sky he turned around and stared at the boys. He heard a "swoosh" as the ball fell through the center of the net behind him.

"Guess I still got it," Justice remarked in a boastful tone.

"Man, we're going to miss you," one of the boys said.

"I'll come back and check on you guys," Justice promised. "Don't think just because I'll be across the country I won't be checking in on you all. This is my city and I have eyes and ears everywhere. You guys are looking good. If you remember to stay in school, get good grades and be respectful to your mothers, you'll have it, too. I promise you that."

One of the boys told Justice that he already does all that, and Justice replied that got him that much closer to his goals.

"Consistency is the key to life. Do it once and you're good. Do it consistently, and you become great." As he walked back into his house, Justice turned around. "Just remember … I *will* be watching, so you best be on your best behavior."

When he got inside, Justice checked his phone and saw a missed call from his ex-girlfriend, Alejandra. The two of them decided to call it quits two weeks ago since he was moving to NYC, and she was still going to be working in L.A. They did not want to maintain the uncertainties of a long-distance relationship. He knew she was very happy in her career, and she did not want to stop him from pursuing this new job opportunity.

Justice called her back to tell her he just returned home from shooting around with the neighborhood kids.

"Aw, I love your relationship with them," Alejandra cooed. "It's cute. I'm glad you aren't like one of these other L.A. douchebags who only cares about the beach, girls and surfing." The phone went silent for a moment before Alejandra continues, "Listen, I know tonight's your last night in town, so I want to take you out for dinner. I have a reservation at Nobu if you could join me."

"I'd love to join you. I have a few errands to run, but I should be able to make it by 6:30 p.m."

They hung up, and Justice got dressed and headed to the barbershop for a haircut. When he pulled up at his barbershop, he saw his barber is just wrapping up with another customer so he decided to stop by the juice bar next door for a smoothie. When he arrived at the juice bar, he saw his friend Samantha and her girlfriend Lissette, who he was also friends with. He walked over, gave them both a hug and asked them how they enjoyed the party.

"We enjoyed ourselves, but I am happier that you enjoyed yourself," replied Lissette.

"And thank you again," Samantha laughed. "You did look surprised. I was almost convinced you didn't know we were having something."

After receiving his smoothie, Justice told the girls that he was getting a haircut and thanked them again for coming last night. He then made his way back to the barber.

"My ex-girlfriend wants to take me out," Justice explained. "I'm not sure what'll happen, but my plan is to go to New York City single."

"Well youngster, in the many years I've been on this earth, the one thing I've come to realize is if you have a dream, don't let anything or anyone stop you from chasing it," offered his barber.

"Thank you," Justice said. "I know it's not going to be easy, but it's the best decision for us. I've been working toward this for most of my life, and I'd be a fool to pass up this opportunity."

After completing his hair cut, Justice headed to the gym, then home.

After waking up from a nap back at his place, Justice began to get ready for his dinner with Alejandra. He shot her a text message to let her know he's on the way and may be a few minutes late. He called for an Uber and when the driver arrived, he told her he's late to a dinner and hoped she could get him there quickly.

At Nobu, he found Alejandra sitting at the bar and walked up to join her. The pair hugged and kissed, and she told him their table should be ready soon.

They stood awkwardly for a minute. Alejandra seemed melancholy. "How was your day, Justice? I'm sure you've been running around all day in preparation for tomorrow."

"Yeah, absolutely. I'm glad you called because I was thinking about you. I love everyone I've met in L.A., but I must admit, I'm going to miss you the most. I really wish we could've continued this, but for me to get to the next step in my career, New York needs to happen."

"I've been thinking about you, too," she confessed. "I wanted us to do this dinner before you left. I know how much your brother means to you. I must admit, I am sad to see you go, but I am also happy to see you so happy. I agree; this is necessary for your career."

The hostess came to escort them to their seats in front of the sushi bar, and they quickly ordered food and drinks. After pacing themselves through appetizers, Alejandra asked Justice what time he will arrive in NYC.

"My flight is supposed to land in Newark Airport in the morning," Justice told her. "My brother is picking me up."

"You know," Alejandra said, "I've heard so much about Walter, but I'm upset I've never met him. I guess I will have to wait until I come to New York."

"Well, I need to confirm details on tomorrow," Justice offered. "Why don't I call him and you can talk to him? It won't be the same as meeting him in person, but it'll have to do for now."

She thought it was is a great idea. After a few rings, Walter finally picked up.

"Why are you taking Justice away from me?"

Justice bit back a laugh until he saw her face change. He inched closer to the phone and overheard Walter say he was just evicted from his apartment and as of now, they don't have anywhere to stay. He quickly grabbed the phone from Alejandra.

"What are you talking about?" Justice exclaimed. "I didn't receive any messages about this."

"Well," his brother explained, "I'm going to stay with my neighbor and sadly, she only has a studio apartment so there's no space for another person. I bet you can find a room at the Andaz on Wall Street, though. They have amazing rooms at great rates."

Justice began to calculate the room rate and the number of nights in his head and asked Walter if he was serious.

"Of course I'm not serious," Walter laughed. "I just wanted you to cut out this silliness. I'll be at the airport to bring you home."

After the call, Justice told Alejandra that Walter was only joking, and everything was fine.

"Can you believe he told me that he was evicted from his apartment and I was going to have to stay in a hotel?" Justice asked.

The pair laughed, watching as their food arrives at the table. "Hey, I have a question for you," Alejandra asked. "Who is Susanna?"

Justice stared at her with a confused look, admitting her he doesn't know anyone named Susanna. "Why do you ask?"

"Well, while calling your brother, you got a text message from a random number and the message said it was someone named Susanna."

Justice then remembered that Susanna was the woman from his party who stayed at his apartment. He told her Susanna was a woman he was introduced to at his going-away dinner the night before. "We spoke a little bit. She's friends with my friend Samantha and ended up staying at my place last night," claimed Justice.

Without saying anything else, Alejandra look at Justice with skepticism and asks him if he was dating her.

"Of course not!" he exclaimed. "I only met her last night and didn't even remember her name until you mentioned it now. She slept over and this morning I could not even remember her name. She was just someone I met. You know I'm focused on New York. I'm not worried about dating."

"I know Justice, and I never wanted to keep you from pursuing your career. Since we broke up two weeks ago, I just can't stop thinking about you. I know you have goals you're working toward, and I don't want to stop you now."

"I appreciate that," Justice told her. "Listen. We made such a great couple, and maybe we can have a future once I get settled. Let's take some time. If we're both available, maybe we can talk about next step."

"I'd love that."

After dinner, Alejandra asked Justice if they could go back to his place for their last night together.

"I wish! My entire apartment is empty," Justice claimed, "and I'm not sure we could even find a place to sit. It's a mess in there. I got rid of a lot of stuff over the weekend and only have a mattress, my laptop and my speakers."

"Well…" Alejandra thought for a moment. "We can go to my apartment instead? I think we need to spend tonight together."

Justice agreed, and they left Nobu.

On the way to Alejandra's apartment, Justice thought to himself how happy he was to be starting fresh in NYC. As much love as he has for L.A. and his friends there, he was ready to start over. Tonight's discussion with Alejandra reminded him how much he was looking forward to hitting the reset button. He reminded himself that he didn't want to jump into a relationship, and plans to focus on work.

When their car pulled up to Alejandra's building, she walked Justice upstairs and as soon as they got in the door, they began kissing. She told him she had something special for him, and they went upstairs into the apartment.

*****

Justice woke up not long after midnight to get dressed and head back to his apartment to grab his luggage and leave the key with the landlord. He kissed Alejandra and told her he'd call when he got to New York. He then headed downstairs to his Uber.

When he arrived at his apartment, he grabbed the remaining bags and did one last sweep of the apartment. When he opened his bedroom closet, a basketball rolled out that he meant to give to the kids the morning before but forgot about. He still wanted to leave it with neighborhood, so he decided to leave them a note reminding them of their promise.

He grabbed a marker and piece of paper and began to write his note. *Don't forget, I'm the reigning champ of this court. Now that I'm leaving, the court is yours, but for you to take the title as kings of the court, you've got to commit and remember what I told you. Stay in school, get good grades and respect your mothers. If you fail to live up to any of these, I will know. I may be in New York City, but my Hollywood Hills still have eyes everywhere. With Love, Justice.*

He then placed the note in one envelope and his apartment keys and proxy card in another. On his way out of the building, he made a stop at the building's rent-drop box and left his key and card. When he arrived downstairs, his transportation was already outside. He told the driver to give him one moment so he could drop off the basketball at the court.

While riding to the airport, Justice left a voicemail for Walter telling him he was on the way. He also realized he wasn't wearing the pendant his parents gave him as a child. He quickly thought back to where he last had it and remembered he had it during the dinner his friends held for him, but not for dinner with Alejandra. He usually never took it off so he was surprised he didn't have it. He was unsure if he had it with Susanna. He attempted to contact her, but she didn't pick up the first two calls. It's not even sunrise, so he figured she was still sleeping, but called again anyway. On the third attempt, she picked up with a groggy "Hello?"

"Hey, I'm sorry to call you so late," Justice said in a rush, "or early, or whatever, but I'm heading to the airport and I can't find my lucky necklace."

"Does it have a butterfly on it? I found it on the floor of the restaurant on the night of your party. Maybe you dropped it? I wasn't sure whose it was but thought it was cute, so I kept it. I've got it in my drawer, but the lock is broken. It must have broken off, and that's it was on the ground.

A relieved Justice told the driver to head to her apartment before the airport. When he arrived at her apartment, she handed him the necklace.

"I'm so glad you had it," Justice said. "I couldn't go to N.Y. without it." Justice looked at his watch, noticing he was almost late for the flight. "Have to run, love, but I'll talk to you soon."

CHAPTER 9:

BEST LIFE

Walter- December 2016

On the early evening of Monday, December 19, 2016, Walter answered his doorbell to find his neighbor, Santina Sanchez, standing there with a grocery bag full of items. They had previously arranged for her to come over to help him clean the apartment and prepare for the arrival of his older brother.

Santina lived down the hall and had known Walter for about ten months. They had been friends ever since. Since they were both young, single professionals with no children, they naturally found themselves connecting regularly.

Walter knew he was a good-looking African American male who maintained his appearance through a healthy diet and regular fitness. Santina was an attractive Latina with a curvy figure and almost angelic profile. She illuminated any room she entered and had a certain talent of forcing others to smile. Because of that, Walter loved having her over.

Unlike many of the women he has dated, he did not have any sexual intentions for Santina. He enjoyed her company and felt he could speak freely around her. When Walter needed a favor, he generally repaid it with another favor. Tonight was an example of that. Santina was helping him prepare for Justice's arrival, so offered to cook dinner. The plan was to open a bottle of Robert Mondavi, and make some chicken and mashed sweet potatoes.

Santina brought over a few ingredients so they could make dessert together. She told Walter she just learned her mother's flan recipe and wanted him to be her taste-tester, to which Walter happily agreed.

As she walked into Walter's apartment, his phone began to ring. The caller ID shows it's Justice calling. Walter ignored it the first time, but Justice called again.

"I'm going to take this in the next room really quick," Walter told Santina. "I'll be right back."

When Walter picked up the call, and heard the voice of a female on the other end.

"Who is this?" Walter asked.

"Why are you taking Justice away from me?" the female replied.

She sounded a little intoxicated, and now Walter can hear Justice laughing in the background, so he decided to play along.

"Did Justice receive my message on Sunday morning about the apartment? I left him a voicemail that I was being evicted at the end of this week. Just want to make sure he's aware so he can start working on somewhere else to stay."

The female told Walter that Justice didn't get the message, but before she could say anything else, Justice grabbed the phone.

"What do you mean you got evicted? I didn't get any messages from you. What are you going to do?"

"Well," Walter drawled, "I was planning on staying with my neighbor, but unfortunately she only has a studio so there isn't any room for you. You should consider staying at the Andaz on Wall Street. They have some really great rates on rooms."

Justice sounded worried, and asked Walter if he was being serious.

"Of course I'm not being serious. I just wanted to get you back for putting that girl on the phone!"

"My bad, bro," Justice laughed. "That was Alejandra. She's so sad about me leaving that she called you from my phone. My flight gets in tomorrow at eleven-thirty in the morning. Will you be there to pick me up?"

"I'll be there. I have company over for dinner right now, so I need to go, but I'll see you in the morning."

During dinner, Walter told Santina that he had some ideas on another fundraiser he wanted to host for the United Way. They had previously spoken about how successful the Skate and Sip event was, and she knew fundraising was a great passion of his.

"Since fundraising is something you enjoy, you'll be successful at anything you choose," she said.

"Thank you," Walter smiled. "My passion for fundraising is only half of the reason why I commit myself. I believe my bigger obligation is to be there for the kids. As a child, I almost lost one of the closest people to me because I didn't feel I had anyone standing in my corner. I had animosity and distrust for my brother because I thought he abandoned me for others. Loneliness and distrust is a dangerous combination for a kid who feels they already don't have anyone looking out for them."

He then told her about the experience in Baltimore and how so many people walked by the robbery and did nothing.

"If it hadn't been for Justice, I would've completely lost faith in humanity. As I stood there with a gun pointed at the back of my head, I closed my eyes because I thought it was over. There were at least a dozen people staring at what was happening and doing nothing at all. Not that I was expecting Superman to swoop down from the sky, but not one person even tried to help. I want to do what I can to ensure no other child feels that level of loneliness and fear. I haven't talked about this in such detail since I was in high school. I guess we can blame the wine for that." Walter shrugged, somewhat embarrassed.

"Thank you," Santina said gently. "I know it wasn't easy to tell a story like that."

They spent the next hour and half making the flan and cleaning the kitchen. Unlike the other women who found themselves in Walters's apartment, Santina could cook, she wasn't afraid to clean and she could talk about things of substance. Walter was very impressed.

"You know," he said, "most women who come over to my home enjoy a free meal as a prelude to great sex. I'm not used to having this level of support from my company. Despite this not being a date, I appreciate you being here."

Despite their fairly new friendship, her personality gave him the courage to be honest and her substance challenged him to think differently. He had only known her ten months, but he felt as though they had been friends for longer, and told her as much.

After finishing their second bottle of chardonnay, the friends decided it would be best for them to leave the dessert for the morning. The decided to watch TV in the living room, which was also where they fell asleep watching *Bad Boys II.* While watching TV, Santina asked Walter what his intentions are.

"Having someone of the opposite sex who you can trust to be honest with you without having any alternative motives is rare," she said.

"I'll be honest with you, Santina, I'm not entirely sure what my intentions are. At this point in my dates, I'm usually undressed and kissing my date. When I invited you over, it was strictly to help me prepare for my brother's arrival. There's something very respectable about you, and I'd like to keep that commitment to keeping it cordial."

"Thank you," Santina said gently. "I appreciate your honestly and love the fact that you're a gentleman. If you would've made a move, I would have had to slap you."

The pair fell asleep watching the movie. Walter woke up in the middle of the night and escorted Santina to his bed, where the two fell asleep.

*****

The next morning, Walter woke up to his alarm ringing and the smell of chorizo coming from his kitchen. He noticed Santina is no longer in bed and figured she must be in the kitchen. He grabbed his robe and made his way to the kitchen, where Santina handed him a cup of coffee and told him to get ready to eat.

"I woke up early to prepare a typical Colombian breakfast: Rice, beans, eggs, arepa, ground beef and chorizo."

Walter wasn't used to waking up to the smell of homemade food since he lived by himself. He told her that most of the time, women who stay overnight are sent home in an Uber before breakfast.

"You're the worst," Santina joked.

They both laughed and Walter joked that he may need to put a ring on it so he can eat like this every day, which made the two chuckle again.

"I can do more than just make a good cup of café bustelo," Santina remarked, throwing him a flirtatious smile.

As the neighbors ate, Santina asked Walter his plans for his brother's visit.

"I know Justice is an independent person," Walter replied, "He calculates each of his moves well in advance. The only significant plans I have for him is a welcome home party, which we'll throw the same time as my big New Year's party."

"Oooh, that sounds exciting."

"Well the party's something I host annually, and every year I feel an obligation to make it bigger than the year before. As always, I'm ready to deliver," Walter said.

As they wrapped up breakfast, Santina began to take care of the dishes, but Walter quickly stopped her.

"Don't lift a finger. The breakfast you prepared was phenomenal and even though I want to run to my room to go back to sleep, it's my turn to clean up. You relax and let me take care of things."

Walter had never eaten like this before so it was a nice treat on the day of his brother's arrival. As he grabbed their plates to put them in the dishwasher, Walter told Santina she has a mighty fine figure for having eaten like that through her childhood.

"Thank you," she replied with a coy smile. "The yoga and Pilates have worked wonders over the years. Also, the salsa dancing has helped tremendously."

As they continued to discuss the upcoming party, Walter told Santina he'd like her to be his plus-one.

"Even with all the clients, managers and celebrities who will be attending," he said, "I only have interest in satisfying two people: you and Justice."

Since they had been neighbors longer than friends, she told him she wouldn't know many of the other people there.

"Don't 'worry," Walter promised. "The party will be fun. There won't be any weirdos."

Santina seemed a little hesitant at first, but finally told him she would love to go.

The two had grown incredibly close in such a short time, and were almost best friends. Walter trusted Santina and considered her his closest female friend. He attributed their bond to the fact that they were both young, ambitious and saw a lot of themselves in each other. But it was more than that.

She told him her only request of him was for him to come with her to the mall to find a dress for the party.

"I love shopping," Santina told him. "I can tell you do, too, because of your fashion sense."

Walter smiled, agreeing to join her in the coming days. "Who would've thought ten months ago, that two strangers would wind up best friends?"

"I think the way we met made us very close, because it was at a very tough time for me," Santina said.

"Is your ex-boyfriend still bothering you?" Walter asked.

"I guess not. He stopped commenting on my Facebook and Instagram pages. He must have found another person to leech off."

CHAPTER 10:

11TH FLOOR

Walter – **February, Ten Months Prior**

That morning, Walter was leaving to go to the gym and do some grocery shopping when he sees a U-Haul truck in front of his luxury apartment building. There were movers in the truck emptying items. He figured another wealthy family was moving in and considered introducing himself later. He left and jogged to the gym, which was located about two miles away from his building.

After leaving the gym and grocery store, Walter decided to walk his regular route home which allowed him to pass by the house of Simon and Sabrina, two children Walter found begging for food on the side of the street one day.

One year prior, Walter was jogging on Marin Boulevard, when he was stopped by a sixteen-year-old boy who begged him to purchase a meal for him and his young twelve-year-old sister Sabrina. Being that Walter already had a soft spot for children in need, he decided to end his jog to treat the children to lunch. During that lunch, Walter learned that the children's mother, Sarahmi, worked as a day-time cashier at a local grocery store. She often found herself accepting overtime shifts in order to provide for Simon and Sabrina. This caused her to be out of the house for most of the day. When Simon explained this to Walter, he instantly decided he wanted to get involved and support the children and their mother. He returned later that day to meet with their mother and to learn more about her story. She was a single mother, and Walter saw an opportunity to mentor the children while supporting the family.

Since that day, Walter decided to make their home a regular stop on his jogging route. He developed a friendship with Sarahmi that allowed her to build a trust in him. The children's father was in prison so she appreciated Walter for providing a strong male presence in their lives. He found himself regularly stopping by with food, clothing and books for the children.

This February morning was no different. The children were at school, so Walter stopped by with groceries for Sarahmi. She was off that morning and offered to cook breakfast for Walter, but he declined because he had to get his groceries back home before they spoiled.

When he arrived back to his building in the early afternoon, he saw the same U-Haul truck was still parked out front, but the truck was now only half-filled. The two movers he saw earlier were sitting at the truck, so Walter asked them if they were still moving the same people in from earlier

"Yes, we moved them in earlier." the guy answered, clearly amused. "Here's the kicker. While we were unloading the truck, the couple got into this huge argument and the woman told us not to unload anything else."

"What floor did they move into?" asked Walter.

"The eleventh," replied the other mover. "My advice, Mister? Stay out of it."

Good advice, Walter figured, except he lived on the eleventh floor himself. "Thank you, guys, for the information. Don't work too hard

When the elevator arrived on his floor, Walter saw a tall gentleman with sleeve tattoos who stomped into the elevator as Walter departed.

Assuming this was his new neighbor, he decided it wasn't the best time to introduce himself, since it seemed like the man was in a rush.

Two days later, Walter was returning from work one evening and saw a Hispanic woman coming from the laundry room and walking toward one of the apartments on the other end of the floor. She was wearing a tank top and tights, and holding a basket full of clean laundry. He had never seen her before and assumed she was the wife of the new neighbor. She introduced herself as Santina Sanchez and said she just moved in.

"Hi Santina," Walter said cheerfully. "It's a pleasure to meet you. I'm Walter Benine from apartment 1124. Are you the new neighbor who moved in with your husband?"

"I did move in a few days ago, but I didn't move in with anyone," she says with a scowl. "I also don't have a husband. The man you are probably referring to is my boyfriend, Malcolm. He assumed he was moving in when I moved here. He even asked the moving company to stop by his mother's place and move his stuff here, too. We got into a big argument that day. I think he finally got the point."

Walter extended his hand and welcomed her to the building. "I've been here for about two-and-a-half years and love it. Everyone keeps to themselves and the staff is friendly. Think you're going to like it here," explained Walter

"Wow, that's awesome! I'm sure I'm going to love it here. All right. Well, I won't hold you any longer."

Walter then turned around and began walking toward his apartment. Santina picked up her basket from the ground and watched Walter walk away.

Just as Santina was about to turn around and walk toward her apartment, the elevator doors opened and Malcolm walked out. Walter saw this and entered his apartment.

Santina

"How did you get back in here?"

Santina was surprised to find her boyfriend, Malcolm, standing in her new apartment building after just telling that new neighbor she would be living alone.

"There's no door that can hold me back," replied Malcolm. "I found a door on the side of the building and came in that way."

"Well, you need to let me know when you're coming," insisted Santina. "You can't just show up to my apartment, because I might not be home. I'm also going to report that broken lock."

As he had gotten off the elevator, Malcolm saw Walter walk into his apartment and now asked Santina who it was.

Santina threw her hands up in frustration. "He was the neighbor. We *just* met in the hallway!"

Santina told herself Malcolm accepted that answer, but she could sense his jealousy has peaked.

They didn't discuss it further, but she knew how jealous Malcolm got over the slightest things.

Walter

Over the next two weeks, Walter overheard the new neighbors arguing regularly. Even though Santina mentioned Malcolm does not live there, Walter got the sense that he was over at her apartment fairly regularly. Fortunately for Walter, they lived at the other end of the hallway so he only heard the couple arguing when he was near the elevator or going to the trash room. In that same time period, he could hear the couple arguing about everything including the various women sending Malcolm text messages in the middle of the night, money being stolen and his lack of employment.

Walter had never officially met him, but from how he seemed in passing, Malcolm was an arrogant, privileged momma's boy who believed he could take whatever he wanted regardless of who he hurt. The fact that Santina told Walter that Malcolm lived at home with his mom meant she believed he was selfish, too. As time goes on, Walter continued to overhear the couple argue every day, but one day it sounded as if thought it had escalated beyond an argument and Walter knew he needed to step in.

One night in early March, Walter returned home from the gym and was welcomed by the typical yelling coming from down the hall. He didn't think it was anything more than one of their regular disagreements, so he was ready to ignore it. As he went for his keys though, he could hear items being thrown and feared this disagreement may have escalated beyond one of the normal yelling matches.

As he approached Santina's door, Walter was hit by the strong smell of alcohol. He heard Malcolm yelling, "Ungrateful bitch! You would still be in the hood if it wasn't for me."

Walter then heard something shatter and quickly entered the apartment through the front door, which was ajar. Upon entering, he saw Santina standing in a corner while Malcolm was yelling and throwing items. He saw the bruise on Santina's arm. Without thinking, Walter walked over to Santina.

"Are you okay?" he asked.

"I'm fine," Santina insisted, even though there were tears in her eyes. "I'm just over that asshole's nonsense. I'm done with him, and I want him to leave forever."

Full of righteous anger, Walter turned to Malcom.

"I need you to leave now. Santina does not want you here."

Malcolm, who was clearly drunk, stood his ground. "Blow me, asshole. Santina's my girlfriend. She and I are just having a disagreement."

Malcolm then approached Walter, but Walter pushed him back. Walter didn't want to get involved from the beginning and certainly did not want to get into a physical altercation.

"Truth be told," he said, "I don't want to fight you, but I will not tolerate disrespect. Watch your mouth, or I'll give you a reason to remember your manners."

Malcolm heard Walters's threat and turned his attention back to Santina. "Is this your new lover? Is this the asshole you've been cheating on me with? I don't care if it is, just tell him to leave so we can talk."

"I don't want anything to do with you!" Santina replied. "I want you to leave and never come back!"

Seeing that Walter wasn't going anywhere, Malcolm attempted to walk over to Santina, but Walter was still standing between them and pushed the man backward again.

A frustrated Malcolm saw Walter was not going anywhere and finally agreed to leave, but not before he told them it wouldn't be the last time they saw his face.

Neither know if this expression was for them and assumed Malcolm thought the entire situation was a joke.

After Malcolm left, Walter walked over to the door and locked it. He walked up to Santina, comforting her with a hug and she began to break down, crying in his arms.

"Malcolm was accusing me of all types of stuff," she sobbed. "He said he knew I was cheating on him with someone else. I'm not. I wouldn't!"

"He's gone now," Walter tried to tell her, but she only shook her head miserably.

"He assumed the real reason I didn't want to see him was because I had someone else over. He called me a cheating, lying bitch and began to yell at me. I can't stand it when he talks to me like that. I didn't let him move into my apartment because he's an alcoholic momma's boy who can't stand on his own two feet."

Just as Walter suspected, he thought to himself.

"Wow. I am so sorry you had to deal with that. It's over now, so you don't need to worry about him any more…"

There was then a banging on the door and Walter and Santina heard Malcolm pleading to be let back in.

"Santina, I'm sorry!" he called out. "I didn't mean to yell at you. I've thought about it, and I want you to know I forgive you for calling me names."

Santina stared at the door in disbelief. "Why won't he just go away?"

Walter thought about the situation. "I have one question for you before I react. Do you plan to ever get back with Malcolm?"

"Never," replied Santina.

"Okay. I'll end this tonight, but I don't want you to make me look like a fool and get back with him. I've seen that story too many times."

Santina nodded her agreement.

Walter answered the door and blocked Malcolm from entering, staring directly into his eyes.

"You aren't welcome in the apartment, or the building. Santina doesn't want to see you, and like she said before, the relationship is over. You need to leave, now."

Malcolm tried to push Walter back, but hardly moved him. Walter grabbed Malcolm by his throat with one hand and his shoulder with the other, and dragged him down the hallway. Malcolm aimed a punch at Walter, but missed. Walter released his grip on Malcom's neck long enough to punch him in the face three times before dragging him into the elevator. Once they arrived on the first level, Walter dragged him across the lobby and shoved him out of the front door.

"If I see you in the building," Walter said in a low voice, "or if I hear that you bothered Santina again, I will call the police."

Malcolm sees the seriousness on Walter's face and told him he won't not bother either of them again. He couldn't get out of site fast enough.

*****

Since that day, Walter and Santina had built a strong relationship and confide in each other about everything. They both live alone, were successfully navigating their careers and were both now single. As time passed, they found themselves getting closer and closer, often relying on each other to keep secrets and gain advice.

It is now the morning of December 20, and Walter's excitement is radiating to fill his apartment. He told Santina he much she appreciated her helping him prepare the apartment for Justice.

"I had so much fun with you last night," Santina told him. "I realize your brother is moving in with you so it may be a little bit harder, but we should hang out like this more often."

"I agree, the night was fun and this morning was a nice way to end."

Walter finished getting dressed and began to think about how perfect their situation is. They weren't dating but had a great time together. Unlike most women, Santina was not pressuring him to do things he doesn't want to do, nor was she making him uncomfortable by ogling his success.

Walter thought to himself how much he was looking forward to continuing to build a strong friendship with her. He even thought about how good of a girlfriend or wife Santina would make. She wanted him to continue to have his freedom and encouraged Walter to live life with his brother. He believed she deserved a man like himself. Someone who would open the car door for her, or walk on the outside of the sidewalk without being prompted to do so.

As he continued to wait, Santina finished getting ready. As she put her hair into a bun at the top of her head, she also began to think about how good of a man Walter was, and how few of them were left.

Living down the hall allowed her to see the various women Walter brought home. Although it may seem as if he is entertaining women in excess, Santina was happy to see he believed in enjoying his life. As a single, good-looking male, he was entitled to date as many women as he wanted.

She then began to wonder why a good man like Walter wasn't married. As she made her way back to the living room, she asked him, "Why is it that you haven't found a girlfriend or wife yet?"

Walter told her that he doesn't feel he's met the right woman yet. "To be honest, most of the women I've dated have been searching for more of a caretaker than a companion. They see my success and lifestyle, and seek further commitment after the first date or so, because they're trying to lock me down. That's usually when I begin to look for the exit.

"I love a woman's companionship, but I won't sacrifice myself or my values to take a woman to bed or have a girlfriend. When the right woman comes, we'll both know it. At that point, I may consider a longer-term relationship."

Santina nodded her understanding. "You're still a catch and any woman would be lucky to have you in their life. You never know. Often times, love comes from the least-expected places."

With that, they were both finally ready and made their way to the elevator.

PART IV
DAYS IN THE EAST

CHAPTER 11:

REASONS WE CARE

Walter

Unlike Santina, Walter wasn't going to work. He had taken the remainder of the week off to be with his brother, who would be arriving soon. During his first week back on the East Coast, Justice would have Walter's undivided attention. Santina and Walter walked downstairs from Walter's apartment to head out of their building. When they reached the front desk, Walter saw his Uber driver in front of the building. Walter and Santina hugged, and she walked toward the PATH train, while he jumped into the waiting car.

The driver asked, "Will your wife not be needing a ride as well, Mister Walter?"

"No," Walter replied, "and she's not my wife, just a friend."

As they drove toward Newark International Airport, the Uber driver looked in the rear-view mirror and said, "The two of you looked stunning together. I would have bet money you two were together. Beautiful people usually attract each other."

Despite his silence from the backseat, the driver's comment was on Walter's mind and he couldn't stop thinking about his time with Santina. For the remainder of their twenty-three-minute car ride, Walter reveled in how perfect life was.

He was thriving in his career, he had great friends, and his best friend—his brother—was coming to stay with him. They were at different points in their lives, but were still the same duo that conquered high school many years before. Now, they were primed to conquer NYC.

When they arrived at the airport, something in Walter made him leave a fifty-dollar tip for the Uber driver. He didn't want to take the money, but Walter insisted, leaving the cash in the cup holder. There was no reason for leaving such a substantial tip, but subconsciously, Walter knew it was because the drive helped confirm something he already knew: He and Santina were a beautiful pair.

As the JetBlue arrivals began filtering through the terminal, Walter saw his brother walking and talking with a beautiful young Brazilian woman. Justice called Walter before he boarded his flight at LAX and didn't mention anything about coming with anyone. Walter knew he must have met her either at the airport or on the plane, which was not unrealistic for Justice.

His brother was still the same smooth-talking ladies' man he remembered from their childhood. As he watched his brother exchange phone numbers with the woman, he became excited all over again. The dynamic duo was back together and were ready to conquer the Big Apple.

As his brother and the woman wrapped up their conversation, Walter watched as Justice gave her a hug and kiss on the cheek, and they walked in opposite directions. She walked toward the taxi pickup, and he began approaching his younger brother.

"I see old habits die hard, old man," Walter joked. "You haven't even taken your luggage out of baggage claim and you're scoring dates." Walter wrapped Justice in a bear hug. "Welcome home, big bro!"

"I never let a good opportunity slip through my fingers," replied Justice, unable to let go of his brother.

As they made their way to the baggage claim, Walter congratulated Justice on the "new opportunity," and told his brother how happy he was to have him home. While waiting on the luggage, Justice brought his brother up to speed on his recently failed relationship and how it ended.

"I was dating this beautiful Mexican girl, Alejandra, for some time, but when I found out I was moving out here, I started to disconnect. I've never been one for long-distance relationships, and she wasn't ready to move out here. We decided it was best to separate but remain friends."

"That's the woman who prank-called me?" Walter asked.

"Ha! Yeah. It was my idea to call you last night because she never had a chance to meet you. Alejandra took me out for dinner and then this morning, I found myself asking if I made the right decision when I arrived at the airport. It wasn't until I got on the plane and met the Brazilian girl you saw me speaking with, that I realized I had!"

After picking up the luggage, Walter called their Uber XL and they proceeded toward the pick-up destination for transport home. While commuting back to Jersey City, the brothers updated each other on life and the welcome-home celebration.

"We've got some exciting plans for New Year's," Walter told his brother. "We have a few things we need to do before."

"Cool bro, I'm ready for my welcome-home party!" Justice began to smile. He was ready to see some old friends and make new ones."

When they arrived at the apartment building, Walter pointed in the direction of the PATH train and told Justice that was what he would use to get in and out of Manhattan. Then they headed upstairs and Walter showed Justice around the apartment he would call home for the next few months. During the tour, Justice asked Walter about his dating life, and if the women in NYC had changed since he was last on the East Coast.

"Dating in NYC has been quite the rollercoaster," Walter explained. "I've met some beautiful women who are crazy, and some sane women who aren't drop-dead gorgeous. I'll admit, I've met many women over the past few years and each of them fall into one of three categories. The 'haves,' the 'have nots' and the 'think they have but really don't and are embarrassing themselves by acting like they have.'"

As Walter thought back on his dating life and the many women he'd been with, his mind again wandered back to Santina.

"To be honest," he said, "there's only one woman who may fall within the 'have' category for me. Not because she has a lot of money, but because she is rich in culture, education and goals. Her name is Santina. You'll meet her at the party."

Justice laughed. "She needs to either come over with some friends right now, or you need to get to pouring us a drink."

"I'm thirsty, so a drink will have to do," Walter said jokingly.

*****

The brothers went all over the place during the next few days, reconnected with old friends, visited various bars and restaurants, and did miscellaneous other things to help Justice with a smooth transition back.

The night of the party, everything was perfect.

In the early-morning hours of January 1st, the streets of New York City were unraveling from the festivities of the night before. Most clubs were announcing last call, while the DJ's prepared for the last song in their set. As the party monsters secured their companions for the night and Uber requestors confirmed pick up locations, Walter was arriving at his favorite 24-hour diner in downtown Manhattan for a meal to end the night with his brother, Santina and friends.

Prior to dinner, they had celebrated the night in a private lounge at Beauty and Essex where friends old and new came to celebrate Justice's return. Walter introduced Justice to Santina, who looked marvelous in the little black dress Walter helped her pick out.

Justice had invited the Brazilian woman from the airport, Ana, who he introduced to Walter and Santina. During their time at the nightclub, the drinks flowed, the hors d'oeuvres were in rotation and smiles and laughter were painted on the faces of attendees. The night progressed exactly as Walter had planned it, and being able to see his brother smiling ear to ear was the greatest benefit to all his planning.

Although it wasn't new to Walter, he worried that his brother may not feel comfortable in a setting so extravagant. Walter had planned to speak with Justice to find out what he thought of the party. Before he could do so, Justice looked at his younger brother from across the room and gave him a thumbs up. This was Walter's confirmation that his brother was enjoying himself.

Santina walked up to Walter with a glass of wine and told him how much she loved the evening.

"I asked the bartender for a glass of red wine and he handed me this. Walter took a sip, and told her it tasted like Malbec.

"It's delicious!" Santina confirmed. "I don't think I've ever had Malbec, but it might be my new favorite!"

Walter smiled at Santina and told her how happy he was to hear she found a new favorite wine. He was no stranger to crafting these memorable experiences and partying into the wee hours of the night, but he wasn't sure if L.A. had changed his brother. After watching Justice across the room and as they left the club, Walter knew his brother had a great time.

As the group made its way into the 24-hour diner, Chateau, Walter was greeted by the host who escorted them to their private space upstairs. Chateau was one of Walter's favorite places in Manhattan because of its hospitality, extensive menu and comfortable accommodations.

As the group made its way into the intimate private space on the second floor, they heard Sade "The Sweetest Taboo" playing on the Sonos speakers, which set the tone for the group. This was the type of mood Walter was used to from Chateau, and he was happy his guests also had a chance to experience the same feeling. The table overlooked the restaurant and had a table minimum of $1,000 per reservation.

Because of the holiday, the minimum for that night was actually $5,000, which Walter agreed to pay because of the event. As they approached their table, Justice signaled his brother to take the seat next to Santina as he sat next to Ana. Justice watched his brother and Santina talk all night during the party and figured it would make sense for them to continue into dinner. Walter sat beside Santina, who was next to Ana and Justice. After the guests were seated, the restaurant manager, Javier, returned to the room and introduced the server to the table.

The young server had never met Walter, but had heard many great stories of his kindness and candor. He arrived with ten champagne glasses filled with Dom Perignon to highlight the New Year's celebration.

As the dinner commenced, Walter saw how comfortable Santina had become with Justice and the rest of the group, and leaned in to thank her.

"For what?" she asked.

"For coming out tonight and enjoying yourself. Everyone loves you and Justice even made a comment about how 'dope' you are, and how I made a good choice bringing you as my date."

"That's good to hear!" Santina smiled. "I'm really enjoying myself and everyone has been so nice. Wasn't sure this was a date. I'm a lady, so a candlelit dinner will have to be our follow-up date. Don't worry about finding a place, 'cause I plan to take *you* out next time."

"Of course," Walter remarked in surprise. "A candlelit dinner sounds perfect."

As the meal portion of dinner ended, Santina leaned in to tell Walter he should give a toast to a successful evening. Walter had considered it earlier in the night, but was still on the fence because at this moment, all the guests at dinner ware heavily intoxicated and probably wouldn't remember anything he said.

At Santina's request, however, Walter decided to give the toast. He ordered two more bottles of Dom Perignon and asked the waiter to fill all the glasses. Once the champagne arrived, Justice asked for the waiter to invite Javier upstairs, so they, too, could join the toast.

"This is typically frowned upon by management, but for the holiday, management allows the staff to enjoy the celebration. I want to first begin by thanking Javier and the team for always accommodating me at the restaurant.

"Next, I'd like to thank all of you for joining the festivities at Beauty and Essex, and extending your night into dinner at Chateau. This year has shown me how hard work can properly be rewarded. I want to encourage everyone to make this next year your biggest year yet.

"I couldn't have selected a better group to come into the new year with. I have so much love for each of you, even though it may not seem like it because I'm drunk."

The crowd laughed and Justice joked that everyone loved him too, and thanked him for playing the "host with the most."

Walter looked at his brother, beaming with pride and continued, "To you, brother, and your new Netflix show."

Justice smiles up at him and raises his glass.

"We used to dream about days like these when we were kids," Walter explained. "We would stay awake for hours just talking about the future. And look at us now. Our parents once sat us down and gave the two of us these pendants we still wear today. My pendant is a bee and his is a butterfly. We were told that these pendants represented the people our parents believed we were.

I wish our parents were still alive so I could tell them they were right. Justice, you are an inspiration, you are my mentor and you are my reason. Despite never saying it, I've always wanted to be the butterfly because I saw how you represent it. When I finally understood what Mom and Dad meant that night, I realized that I wanted to be just like you. I could go on for hours about this guy, but I'll leave you with one quick story instead.

"One time, when I was in the sixth grade, another student jokingly told me my skin complexion was as dark as it was because my ancestors were out in the sun too long. At the time, I was well aware of slavery, so I knew what the student was referring to. This was one of the first times I was picked on by another student, so I took it very badly.

"When Justice heard what the other student said, he told me that the truth was we were the descendants of African kings, and the reason for our dark-skinned complexion was because of the melting pot of different knowledge, culture and skill sets that went into our ancestry. Just like when you mix all primary colors and get black, these attributes were mixed together to build kings and queens.

"At the time, I didn't absorb the advice, but in time, it slowly helped turn a helpless, shy, timid adolescent into a confident leader who understood his worth. Thank you, Justice."

As he thanked his friends for joining, Walter couldn't stop looking at Santina, who was staring back at him in amazement. She knew Walter was a confident, free thinker who knew how to control a room, but she had never seen this vulnerability in him. As a human resource professional, she was used to dealing with individuals who were confident, which often translated into either modesty or arrogance.

Everyone else she dealt with was sensitive, which in turn caused them to be very vulnerable and shy.

Never had she met anyone who she felt represented both traits equally…until now. The enigma that was Walter Benine found himself at the pinnacle of her interest, and she wanted to learn more.

Despite her mental strength, Santina knew she was more vulnerable than confident. She knew she needed a strong partner to help her find her confidence. She was beginning to believe Walter might be that partner.

As the two of them gazed at each other and smiled, Walter asked everyone to raise their glasses.

He yelled, "Prost!," a popular German remark for celebration.

They all clinked glasses at the center of the table and drank their champagne. As the night came to an end, Santina, Justice and Walter shared an Uber XL home. Before they left Chateau, Justice and Ana spent a few minutes talking before she got in her own Uber and headed home. Their Uber XL pulled up next, and the group got in. During their trip home, Santina told the boys she would edit the pictures from the night and share them in an email later in the week so they could post them on their Facebook pages.

"I'm just ready to get home, take off these heels and my bra and go to sleep," she said.

"Me too!" joked Justice. "I don't start filming until later in the week, so I may not wake up until then."

When they arrived at the apartment building, Justice headed straight to the apartment while Walter walked Santina to hers at the opposite end of the hall.

"Thank you for an amazing night. Everyone was so nice and you were such a gentleman throughout the night," she said.

She began to turn around to enter her apartment. As she unlocked the door, Walter knew it might be his only opportunity, so he pulled her back to his body and gave her a kiss on the lips.

They finally pulled apart smiling, wished each other a good night and went inside their respective apartments.

CHAPTER 12:

LOVE YOU FROM A DISTANCE

Justice- January – February 2017

On the first Thursday of 2017, Justice began filming for the show. Since he had a few days between the New Year's party and first day of filming, he spent his days rehearsing his lines to fully immerse himself in the role. There were a lot of people committed to his success, so he wanted to ensure he does not disappoint anyone who's invested in him.

The show was rated very favorably with focus groups and critics so he knew the pressure and anxieties that came due to his starring role were normal.

Besides play practice, he began speaking more and more with Ana over the coming days. They learned so much about each other in the days following the party. They spoke every day, and their friendship quickly began to grow into a relationship.

Back in December, when Justice decided to end the relationship with Alejandra, he told himself it was so he could focus more on himself and his work. His goal was to start fresh and avoid any commitments that would take his attention away from his work.

As he found himself spending more time with Ana, he realized he was jumping from one relationship to another. He was not upset about this, and told himself that this was just the way life happened.

As the next few weeks passed by, Justice and Ana began seeing each other more and more. They agreed to wait on committing to an official relationship, but also agreed that they would be exclusive.

On the plane ride from L.A. to Newark Liberty, he learned she was a model who lived in NYC, traveled often for work. She had an apartment in Union Square and her agency was in Soho. He knew that her work required her to travel like Walter's, so he didn't want to commit to an obligation neither one of them could fulfill.

Since the New Year's party, the pair spent a significant amount of time meeting in the city and Justice even found himself staying with her often in her apartment. The show was filming in downtown Manhattan, so it was very convenient for him to commute from her apartment instead of Walter's.

The first month of filming was excellent. Justice felt like he was around people who wanted to see him succeed, and the show had the backing to drive success. Due to their connections to Christopher Nolan, Hans Zimmer and others in the film industry, the producers had many resources at their fingertips to create a hit.

Justice saw this as one of the greatest benefits and was ecstatic because he knew he thrived in this type of environment. A healthy budget, a free-thinking forum, and a reliable crew allowed for a creative and flexible working environment, both for Justice and the other actors on the show.

After the New Year's party, Walter spent a lot of time with Santina. When he was not working or out with Santina, he found time to hang out with Justice. As Justice was also now dating Ana, the brothers worked efficiently to coordinate schedules. In the beginning of February, they found a few nights to visit sporting events, which were usually followed by dinner and drinks in the city. They were both Knicks and Yankees fans, so when they could, they caught as many games as possible.

*****

On the morning of Friday, February 10th, Justice woke up to a text message from Walter.

Hey Jus, I'm heading to the Park Hyatt for Valentine's weekend with Santina. The apartment is all yours if you need.

Justice replied, **<3 =)**

Justice then turned over to see Ana still sleeping. She didn't have anything to do very early like he did, so he quietly got out of bed and began getting dressed for work. The next few days were spent with Ana and on the set.

*****

On the morning of February 13, 2017, Justice checked the mailbox and saw he finally received the second installment of his signing bonus for the Netflix drama in the mail. Per his contract, the first installment was paid upon signing and the second half was to be paid after his first 45 days of filming. He was excited to receive the remaining balance because his bank account saw a severe drop during his move to the East Coast.

Being that he lived with Walter, he put his younger brother's address on everything, including his contract, checks and bank accounts. Unfortunately, due to his procrastination, Justice never got around to arranging direct deposit so each time the production company issued a paycheck, it was sent in the mail to their shared Jersey City address. Waking up to this made Justice so happy that he decided to send his younger brother a text message and tell him he would pay rent this month.

Hey Walt, finally got the rest of my money from my signing bonus. Thanks for everything you've done for me so far. As a token of my gratitude, I'll pay the full balance of rent this month.

There was a shared bank account between the brothers which they used to pay rent and other things for their apartment. When Justice arrived on the East Coast, they created the shared account in his name.

After showering and getting dressed, Justice went to grab the check book so he could take care of the rent. When he went to their cabinet in the living room, he noticed his checkbook was missing.

Did you move the checkbook anywhere?

Walter responded, ***Sorry, Justice. The checkbook is in my overnight bag in my closet. I must have forgotten to unpack it.***

Justice went to Walter's room and found the checkbook right where Walter said it would be. He filled out a check for their rent and headed downstairs to drop it off at the management office.

*****

After leaving the office, Justice sent Alejandra a text message to see how she was doing.

Hey Alejandra – long time. Just checking in to say hi. We haven't spoken in a while so I wanted to see how you are.

Alejandra responds, ***Hey Babe – I'm great. I miss you so much.***

Awww. Yeah, it has definitely been a long time. I actually started dating someone from here. She is a model.

Ohh.

Yeah as you know it was not my intention but it kind of just happened. We met, hit it off and have been hanging out since. I wanted to be honest with you from the beginning.

I appreciate that. Are you happy?

Yes, very happy. I hope you found someone special, too. Again, just wanted to say hi. Take care of yourself.

I will. You too. Even though we aren't together and don't see each other like before, you should always know that I'll love you from a distance.

Justice then continued with his day before arriving to the TV set in the early afternoon. When he arrived, he sent Ana a smiley face emoji and told her how happy he is.

Hey! Hope you're having a good day, Love. Just wanted to let you know I was thinking about you.

Justice then began filming and when he returned to his phone he saw an unread message from Ana.

Miss you honey. Can't wait to see you later!

CHAPTER 13:

MOMENTS IN TIME WHEN THE CLOCK STOPS

Walter – January – February 2017

After the events of his New Year's party, Walter knew he needed to acknowledge the kiss he and Santina shared and the feelings he was beginning to have for her. What began as a regular friendship between two neighbors was now becoming something more serious.

Since helping Santina kick Malcolm out of her apartment almost a year ago, Walter felt he and Santina have become very comfortable with each other. After that situation, they found themselves relying on each other for general advice and overall support. They had discussed everything: work, finances, politics… everything.

Although the night before Justice moved back home was one of the first times they'd hung out, they both felt very comfortable with each other. Something about the chemistry of the evening began to bond their energies. From that night to the party, Walter thought about Santina often, but could not muster the courage or find the opportunity to address it. How could he deliver a proposal to a boardroom full of executives with ease, but find it challenging to express his true feelings to a woman like Santina?

He was happy he finally found the opportunity and courage to kiss her on New Year's morning. He didn't regret a second of it. But now it was time to discuss their future.

On the first day back to work, Santina and Walter agreed to meet at eight in the morning at a café in the city for breakfast before heading to work. Because his client had a headquarters based in Silicon Valley, Walter planned to be in the city very early to launch an advertisement at 5 a.m. ET to ensure it was up by 2 a.m. PT.

Since they were meeting at eight, Walter and Santina decided to meet at Bouchon Bakery, near Santina's office.

Santina arrived before Walter and grabbed a table in the front. When Walter arrived, he handed Santina a picture of the two of them from New Year's and told her it was one of the only pictures he had of her that night.

"I found it in my phone in the morning and instantly fell in love. I was going to send it to you, but figured it may be a nice surprise to print it and frame it."

"Aww, that is so sweet of you. I still have to send you the pictures I took," remarked Santina with a smile.

They began the discussion by talking about how fun the evening was.

"Everything from the party at Beauty and Essex to the nightcap at dinner went off without a hitch," Walter said. "I couldn't have planned for the night to go any better than it did. The next morning, Justice and I sat around the house all day and recovered by watching TV and ordering all our meals through

Grubhub. We also sent out thank-you messages to everyone.

"Wow!" remarked Santina. "I'm sure they were very appreciative of the invitation and of your thank-you message."

After an awkward pause, Santina looked into Walter's eyes. "I guess we also should address the kiss."

"Yes, I suppose we should." Walter rubbed nervously at his face.

"To be honest, that was the best first kiss I've ever had in my life, and I feel like it was a bit overdue. I don't know about you, but I've wanted to do that since you helped me kick my jerk ex-boyfriend out.

"My Abuelita once told me not to waste my time with a man who doesn't give me butterflies in my stomach when he enters the room. Not only did I have butterflies that night, I also felt chills in my entire body when we kissed.

"My grandmother never led me astray before, and I'm happy to report that she did not fail me now." Santina looked into Walter's eyes with genuine affection.

Walter found himself grinning ear to ear. "I've also wanted to kiss you for the longest time but, like you, I wanted to ensure we weren't rushing into anything. You'd just came out of a messy relationship, so I didn't want to be your make-up guy. I'm glad we waited, because our friendship grew. Something about your personality intrigues me. I think it's because you have a lot of ambition, intelligence and you're building your own.

"I guess the next step is to talk about what comes next for us.

"As a leader at my agency, I'm expected to visit client sites regularly after signing a contract," Walter began. "This is Karot's way of onboarding new clients to the agency. I think I have some upcoming travel but would love for us to get together as often as we can. Fortunately we live in the same building, so I think we'll be able to see each other fairly often."

"That makes sense. My work has provided me with a fairly consistent schedule. I would love to see you also, but I understand how much your work means. I want us to invest in something long-term, so I'm willing to adjust to the demands of your schedule." Santina finished, reaching across the table to grab Walter's hand.

Wow. Walter thought to himself. *Santina is caring* and *compassionate. I've hit the jackpot.*

They made their way from the café and when they got to the exit, the pair hugged and went their separate ways.

As he made his way to the subway, Walter began thinking about how he had never met a woman who made him feel the way he did when he was with Santina. Unlike the other women in his life, Santina gave him a reason to want to come home every night. Even if they saw each other for a just a moment, the time spent together was special.

When he wasn't with her, he couldn't stop thinking about her. When he *was* with her, he found himself lost in their time together. He loved the fact that she appreciated culture. Coming from a Colombian upbringing meant she also valued family. This was very important to Walter.

When she arrived at work, Santina also began to think about all the things she loved about Walter. She loved the fact that he was driven, respectful and truthful. All his volunteer work showed how much he cared for others. The fact that he used his resources to impact the world for the better showed how much he understood his duty to the betterment of others.

*****

That night, Santina invited Walter for dinner. When he arrived, Walter handed her a bottle of wine and leaned in for a kiss.

Santina looked at the bottle of wine and flashed him a huge smile of appreciation.

"Thank you!" remarked Santina. "You remembered Malbec was my new favorite. Thank you so much. That was very sweet of you. Dinner should be ready shortly.

"You're too kind. I know it's very early for us, but I figure it might be smart to ask the question now versus later.

"How is it that a man like you hasn't found someone special yet? Do you have a crazy side you're hiding?"

Walter looked into Santina's eyes and began laughing.

"That seems to be the million-dollar question." Walter said. "It's a pretty common question that I receive from everyone. My answer has typically been because the girls I've met have all been crazy or into me for the wrong reasons. I met a woman last year who I thought would be different. She seemed so cool at first, but after a while I got a strange vibe from her. The more we talked, the more I noticed signs of someone seeking a man to take care of her instead of a partner. Not that I do not mind taking care of someone but I don't want to be in a relationship with someone who depends on me, my money and success. I had to cut her off after that.

"You're absolutely right." Santina responded. "You take care of so many other people, I wonder how many people take care of you."

"That's an interesting statement. I guess I've never thought about it before since I never really found myself needing someone else. There was the one situation in Baltimore that required me to need Justice. Strangely, I feel that because he was there for me, I sort of have a debt to be there for him. Not that he said this but it's just a feeling I can't seem to shake. He's the only living person I can say takes care of me.

"Your question brings up a good point that I've never thought about before. Who takes care of me? One night earlier in the year, I was walking down the street and an old man told me there was some emptiness he saw in me based on him looking into my eyes. Maybe he was referring to the fact that I don't have a lot of people taking care of me. I don't really know.

"Before I could ask the old man about it, he disappeared. Despite my skepticism about that moment, I've tried to identify all things in my life that might cause emptiness. For the longest time, I was unable to identify the root of it. I'm successful in my career, have made a lot of money over the years and have a strong relationship with my brother and friends. If you ask me, I'd say I have everything I need.

"It wasn't until the morning after you first stayed over that I considered the thing that may have been missing from my life was a significant other I could call my equal. In the moments we spent together that night, it was as if the clock stopped, which didn't concern me.

"As strange as it seemed, I was happy to be lost in those moments. Most of the girls I dated in the past lacked ambition and were just looking for someone to take care of them. This deterred me from moving forward. My parents raised me to be a protector, but my brother helped me understand my value to a relationship. I sort of feel complete, but that's just my theory."

Santina admitted to dating jerks for most of her life, which caused her to feel like she was doomed to fall for a crook, cheater or bum.

"The circumstances of my childhood and the realities of the environment exposed me to tough truths about life. I didn't want life in that urban neighborhood to be the reality I was stuck with. Despite my goals of a better life, I still didn't have any luck with men.

"Like I said the other night, you are truly a good man. You actually may be the first guy I've met who doesn't creep me out. Most times I am able to see through ulterior motives, and with you I don't see any.

"I'd really like to pursue something with you, and I hope you feel the same way." Santina finished. "If we decide to get together, I have three requests of you. If you agree to them, I think we can work on something more serious. First, always be honest with me. Even if the truth might seem like it will hurt, I still want to know. Second, always challenge me to be better. I want to be with a man, not a boy. I deserve my equal and want someone who will help me fill the holes within myself. Finally, give me a love that's unconditional. I want the parameters of our relationship to have no boundaries. I want us to defy the odds to make it beautiful. If you can agree to these, I'm ready," Santina stated.

"I'll happily commit to that. If I may, I'd also like to add one more to that list," Walter found himself getting excited over the proposition of being together. "Fourth, we should commit to respecting ourselves and this relationship. Never sacrifice or compromise your integrity to appease others, especially me. You're an amazing woman who deserves the world."

The pair agreed to lock each other down and not date anyone else, agreeing to commit themselves to a relationship.

*****

Over the next two weeks, Walter was on the road six out of fourteen days. In his free moments, he communicated with Santina via phone and email to give her updates on his travels, and inquire how her day went.

One evening, in the end of January, during one of their regular FaceTime exchanges, Walter told Santina that he had a scheduled trip at the end of January that he was moving up a week, and that the trip would be his last for a while. Walter could see Santina's smile from his end of the phone.

"I wanted to keep this a secret, but there's another reason I decided to reschedule my work trip.

I picked up two orchestra tickets to see *Hamilton* on Broadway for the weekend before Valentine's Day, and I'd like you to join me."

Originally, Walter hadn't planned on having other plans besides the Broadway show, but decided he wanted to make their first Valentine's Day special, so he planned a weekend to remember.

During the first two weeks of February, Walter and Justice also found time to hang out and enjoy the luxuries Manhattan had to offer. They took in sporting events and dined in various restaurants. The brothers were now in relationships, but they still made it a point to find time for each other when they weren't with their significant others.

*****

As the second week of February commenced, Walter and Santina reconfirmed they'd taken that Friday off. Their plan was to treat themselves to a spa day before going to see *Hamilton* on February 10th.

They knew they didn't need to do anything extravagant to feel secure in their relationship, but thought it would be a nice treat to get away from their normal lives, if only for an extended weekend. Walter also reserved a suite at the Park Hyatt, New York, and had a car scheduled to pick them up from their apartment building that Friday morning.

*****

That morning, Walter woke to the smell of fresh coffee. Santina woke up earlier than Walter and decided to make Colombian coffee for the pair. This forced him to jump out of bed and begin getting dressed. As they got ready, Santina had Carlos Vives blasting on the Sonos speakers in Walter's apartment, and was dancing in her underwear. *Thank goodness Justice stayed out with Ana last night,* Walter thought to himself with a chuckle. When Walter got to the kitchen and saw Santina, he approached her with an excited gesture.

Something about that moment prompted Walter to grab the hands of his love and begin dancing salsa. For the next twenty minutes, their bodies moved in sync as if they were making love. Walter's ability to be playful at any given moment, and Santina's culture made each of these sporadic moments special. After the song ended, Santina told Walter she had something for him. She went into her bag and pulled out a copy of a framed picture of the two of them from the New Year's party. She told him she wanted to get a picture for him, too.

"Wow, this is such a great picture of us. You looked so beautiful that night. You bring out the best parts of me, and I love you for that. I'll hang the picture twice. First in the front of my heart, and second, here in my apartment," Walter explained.

While smiling, Santina reached in to kiss Walter.

Walter then returned to packing their bags as Santina finished getting ready and packed their coffee to go. As their scheduled Uber Black arrived, the couple rushed downstairs to start their weekend.

Justice and Ana were now also dating, so he spent a lot of his time at her place when not with Walter. On the way out, Walter sent his brother a text to let him know they were leaving for the weekend and the apartment was all his. Justice replies with a heart and smiley face emoji.

As they pulled up to the hotel, they were greeted by an elderly bellman who opened the car door for Santina and began unloading their luggage. The bellman escorted them to the reception desk where they were greeted with two glasses of champagne and a warm hello.

Walter had previously arranged for the romance package when reserving his room, but mentioned that it was a surprise so the staff could use their discretion during check in. For that reason, the front desk checked them in as if they were confirmed in a regular reservation and made no mention of the upgraded room or added amenities.

When they arrived at their room, the bellman unlocked the double doors, handed the couple their keys and wished them an excellent stay. Upon entry, they were greeted by a large foyer and a welcome card from management. The foyer led to an open-concept living-room-and-kitchen combo. To the left, they saw another set of double doors that led to the bedroom and en-suite bathroom.

The kitchen had a bottle of Armand de Brignac champagne on ice, and their bed was covered with rose petals. In the bathroom were two bathrobes with their names on them. Santina kissed Walter and thanked him for making this weekend so special.

Almost immediately after they kissed, there was a knock on the door. When Santina opened it, there was a young blond lady in the doorway with a big smile on her face. She introduced herself as Heather, their personal concierge for the weekend, and welcomed the couple to the hotel. She provided her cell phone number, and informed them she would escort them to their spa appointment if they were ready.

After the spa, Walter and Santina went back upstairs to get dressed. Their tickets for the show were for 8:00 p.m., so they had about two hours to get ready and make their way to Richards Rodgers theater for *Hamilton.*

After they finished getting ready, Walter sent Heather a message to ask her to make them dinner reservations after the show. Five minutes later, Walter received a message on his phone.

You are confirmed for a table for two at the NoMad Restaurant at 10:30 p.m.

As they made their way down Seventh Avenue, they noticed a group of street performers putting on a show in the middle of Times Square. Walter looked at his watch. It was 7:15 p.m., so they have enough time to stop and watch.

When Walter and Santina made their way closer to the performers, Walter commented on how they look like they could be a family. There was a strong resemblance in the children and parents, as the two children look like a mix of the African American man and the pale white woman. The older man was playing the drums using a set of buckets, and the older woman was playing a keyboard. The young girl had a saxophone, and the young boy held a violin.

Walter and Santina watched silently, caught up in the beautiful music. The crowd grew and grew until it had completely surrounded the performers.

For the next 20 minutes, the couple found themselves lost in the music. Times Square was filled with onlookers, most who had their cell phones up to film the spectacle. When the group ended a song, Santina and Walter walked up to leave a tip in their jar.

"That was beautiful. Thanks for that. Who are you?" Santina asked the woman.

"We're just a family who was raised and connected through music. My husband used to be a school music teacher but is now retired, and I work as ballet instructor to support the family. We play as a family at night after work and school. The children go to school during the week, so we only get to play together on some Friday and Saturday evenings. And since we're a single income home, my entire salary goes toward essential expenses. All the money we raise out here goes toward the children's college funds and school fees."

"I'm very impressed with how the kids remained composed and had fun despite all the people who showed up. Times Square is typically a place where people are always on the go, so the fact that you were able to stop so many of them was incredible," gushed Santina.

They thanked the family again, and headed to the theater for the show. On the way, Santina commented on how happy she was to meet the family and listen to their music.

"I agree. There was something very special about that family," Walter said.

"It's amazing to see that kind of sacrifice made by the parents. To perform nightly for their children's future is very inspiring. It makes me so happy to see that people like that still exist," Santina said, smiling and grabbing Walter's arm.

When they arrived at the theater, Walter sent Heather a text, asking her to meet them him.

I'm on my way. Will be there in about 10 minutes.

As they get settled in their seats, Heather sent Walter a text to let him know she was at the entrance. Walter kissed Santina on the head before excusing himself to go downstairs to meet her.

In the lobby, he gave Heather an envelope with instructions for delivery. He reiterated his request for discretion, and thanked her for her help.

Walter and Santina continued to dinner after the show then headed back to the hotel to enjoy the remainder of their weekend.

PART V
’TIL DEATH DO US PART

CHAPTER 14:

THE PEOPLE WE COULD NOT SAVE

Walter

Two months after the Valentine's Day weekend, Walter and Justice found time to connect. They met in Midtown Manhattan on a late April night with plans to catch up over drinks before heading to dinner. Seven o'clock in the evening is their target and Haven Rooftop is their destination. So far, 2017 has been excellent for the brothers so they were doing everything they could to enjoy their time together.

When they arrived, they checked in downstairs with the staff before heading upstairs. Walter was a Rooftop regular, and he made sure to say hi to the staff anytime he visited. Their night consisted of laughs, drinks and plenty of conversation before heading to Giorgio's of Gramercy for dinner.

When they arrived at Giorgio's, Walter's phone rang repeatedly but he couldn't hear it. Walter had placed the phone in the breast pocket of his suit jacket, which sat on the back of his chair. He wanted to give Justice his full attention, so he had turned his ringer off.

When he went to the restroom, he finally noticed he had eight missed calls and two voicemails from Santina. He immediately began to worry because it was not like her to call so many times.

When he called back, she didn't answer, so he listened to one of the voicemails. Hitting play, he heard a frantic Santina begging for help.

"Walter, help me. Malcolm showed up at my apartment drunk again and started banging on my door. I'm inside the bedroom now, but I'm scared. I get so scared when he's drunk. I called the cops, but I don't know where they are. It sounds like he's got other people with him, too."

As the voicemail ended, Walter raced back to Justice to tell him they had to leave immediately. Walter went out to hail a cab as Justice settled their tab. When the cab pulled up, they jumped in and Walter told the driver there was an emergency at home.

"Run every red light. I'll pay for any speeding tickets you get. I need to get there, now! Walter dropped a few hundred dollars over the man's shoulder. "Step on it!"

The driver saw Walter's panic and stepped on the gas.

When the driver arrived at Walter's building, they were greeted by police cars and barricades. There were two ambulances and yellow caution tape in front of the building. Walter informed the police officers he and his brother were residents and needed to get upstairs. They allowed him access to the building and advised him to go straight to his apartment. When he arrived on the 11th floor, he ran to Santina's apartment and saw blood on the floor by the entrance. He froze in his tracks, noticing the door frame was damaged as though someone had kicked it in. There were two bodies under white sheets in the living room and Walter instantly dropped to his knees.

As Justice came in behind him, he tried to stop his younger brother from going any farther into the apartment. It didn't matter: Walter was determined and shrugged his brother off. He slowly got up, walked in and asked one of the officers what happened.

"There was a break-in and a homicide," the officer answered, looking at Walter with concern.

Once again, Walter found himself on his knees. *How could this happen*? He swore he would always be there for Santina and in her most vulnerable moment, he wasn't there.

An officer reached down and touched Walter's shoulder. "Sir, I'm going to have to ask you to leave. This is a crime scene."

"I have to see her," demanded Walter.

"Sir, I'm afraid-"

"Just pull back the sheet."

The officer was reluctant at first, but saw the fear in Walter's face and relented. When the officer pulled back the two white sheets in the living room, Walter saw two men whom he did not recognize.

One of the men had a gunshot wound to his head, the other had two gunshot wounds to his chest. Momentarily relieved, Walter instantly began to think of alternative situations that may have resulted in Santina's escape.

He was hopeful she made it somewhere safe, but wasn't sure how. If she made it out, he needed to make sure she was okay.

"Where is Santina? The resident. Where is she?"

The officer was confused, but another overhears the conversation and informs them there were two more bodies in the bedroom. One of them may be the resident.

Walter's heart dropped to the bottom of his stomach. All hope he had suddenly faded, and he once again assumed the worst. As he walked into the bedroom, he saw two bodies on the bed. They weren't yet covered, and he recognized the first body as Santina's. Her beaten, lifeless body was covered in blood.

Beside her was Malcolm, with his pants around his ankles. There is an empty bottle of tequila on the ground with a gun beside it.

"It appears the female was raped and beaten before the male shot her in the head. From the looks of it, it seems the male may have also shot the two others in the front before killing himself. Forensics should confirm everything. Do you know the victim, sir?" asked the officer.

"No, I don't. I'm just the neighbor."

Walter's worst fears are now reality. His shock and fear prevented him from giving the officers any details of their relationship. No matter what he told the police, Santina would be gone forever. Malcolm came back and killed her. He didn't think it was essential for them to know they were dating. Time stood still, and Walter stood at the entrance of their once-shared bedroom, willing the universe to change its mind.

"We should leave," whispered Justice, as he grabbed Walter and attempted to pull him out of the apartment.

Walter told Justice that he needed air, so the pair headed downstairs. When they arrived at the entrance of the building, Walter noticed many reporters were now on the scene, attempting to get a shot of the situation. One reporter in particular was very aggressive, trying to get into the building and trying to get interviews with the police.

Walter overheard her tell a police officer she was a family member of the victim, which Walter thought was false. When she was alive, Santina spoke about her family often and never spoke about having a family member who worked as a reporter. After thinking about it, he convinced himself that he did not want the reporter to interview anyone who didn't really know Santina. Something about what was occurring in that moment compelled Walter to approach her.

"I knew the woman who was killed, and I'm willing to be interviewed. Before we start though, I have one question. Are you really related to her?" Walter questions.

"I'm not related. I didn't even know her." replied the reporter. "I heard what happened and it hit home for me. Domestic violence has always been a sensitive subject for me, and when I heard there was a murder, I got fed up and knew I had to do something. I lied to the officers because I don't trust other reporters to cover this story the way it needs to be covered.

"I've seen these kinds of stories disappear at the bottom of the active case files because of their frequency. The fact that the perpetrator killed himself is even worse, because that means there will be no justice for the woman," the reporter stated.

"Thank you for your honesty and thoughtfulness, but please keep in mind that lying about the dead for a story is inexcusable. I'll help you get the story out there, because I owe that to Santina. She was my girlfriend, and I want you to promise this story appears in print, because her death will mean nothing if nothing comes from this tragedy," demanded Walter.

She nodded her head in agreement and pointed her camera at Walter. "What happened tonight?"

"Based on the information I received, the woman was murdered by her ex-boyfriend in what seemed like a violent outburst fueled by jealousy, rage and alcohol. Three men broke into the apartment and raped and shot the victim." Walter began, voice shaking. "She was a kind and caring soul who was always interested in highlighting the best parts of people. She was playful and full of life, and it's horrible that anyone would want to take her life like this. I wish my sweet Santina eternal peace in heaven, and I will love her forever."

"Why do you think it happened?" asked the reporter.

"To be honest, I don't know all details, but I do know that they were in a relationship that ended about a year ago," Walter replied.

"Did you know the perpetrator? What was your relationship to him?" the reporter asked.

"I didn't know him at all. He was around when she moved in, but not long after that she broke up with him and kicked him out. He threatened her and stalked her social media, but I would never have thought he'd do something like this."

In an unusual occurrence, Walter began to break down and started tearing up on camera. The reporter cut the filming and thanked Walter for his strength and taking the time to speak with her. Justice walked him off the scene and steered him back toward their apartment.

After Walter left the scene, the reporter asked the camera crew to begin rolling again. When they began filming, she looked directly at the camera and in a touching statement, she used the next 60 seconds to address her viewers. The reporter began by asking all victims of domestic violence to speak out against their abusers.

"Your voice is your strongest weapon against the predators who get off on harming innocent women. We may not always have the physical strength to protect ourselves, but together we have a voice that can shake up this city. Tonight's unfortunate occurrence should serve as a reminder that your voices must be heard for change to come. How many more stories must we hear like this one before we act? How many more mothers, sisters, daughters and wives must be damaged or traumatized before we say enough is enough? We hear too many stories of women being mistreated or taken advantage of, and I would like to remind you…we will not stand idle.

"Fortunately, the coward of tonight's occurrence took his own life, but that didn't come without tragedy. I'm sure he couldn't bear to look at himself in the mirror any more after what he did to the victim. To those who are still fighting quietly, please reach out to 1-800-888-4400. If you are battling silently, I want to be your helping hand."

CHAPTER 15:

DON'T LOOK BACK

Walter

As they arrived at the apartment, Walter cannot stop crying and began hyperventilating from the shock. Justice hasn't seen this kind of fear and vulnerability from his brother in many years, and knows it is best for him not to be alone.

"Let's stop here and take a minute. I want you to take a minute and breathe, Walter." Justice spoke in a low, steady voice.

Justice tapped his brother's back as he caught his breath. After a few minutes, Walter got his breath back so Justice led him back to his bedroom to get some rest. When they arrived at Walter's bedroom, Justice told Walter how powerful it was for him to give the interview.

"There are millions of people around the country who will see that story and be able to see Santina for who she really was. Your testimony was amazing, and Santina is looking down from heaven smiling," Justice offered.

"Thank you, Justice. The only reason I agreed to speak on camera was because I figured that reporter wasn't going to tell a story like Santina deserved. I wanted her name to bring as much happiness to the world as she brought to me. She was an angel and with all the fake news these days, the last thing I need is for someone to misconstrue her story or use her name to boost ratings."

Justice helped his younger brother into bed and pulled up a chair to sit nearby until Walter fell asleep. As he lie on his bed, Walter asked Justice why he thought Santina's ex-boyfriend killed her.

"Her ex-boyfriend was nefarious and was battling demons. He was her ex for a reason, but he couldn't see himself without her. When she left him, she probably took the only meaning his life had," Justice offered.

Walter's crying slowed. Through ragged breath he said, "The first time I met her ex-boyfriend, Santina told him to leave her apartment and never come back. He left, but not before threatening us. I regret not taking it more seriously. I assumed he was just upset because he was asked to leave her apartment.

"To be honest with you, I think the trigger that set tonight off might have been social media. Since New Year's, she'd shared pictures of her and I on her pages, and on Valentine's Day, she shared one picture on Instagram and captioned it, "My LOVE."

"He probably went through her accounts and saw how much time we were spending together. She told me he was jealous to begin with, so the pictures probably sent him over the edge."

Justice didn't know Malcolm, but based on how Walter described him, Justice assumed he was right.

"I'm okay now. If it's all right with you, I just want some privacy to clear my mind before bed," Walter claimed.

Against his better judgment, Justice agreed and leaves the room.

Walter lie on his bed thinking about the day. He remembered that Santina had left him two voicemails, but he had only listened to the first one. As he played the second one, he could hear Santina arguing with her ex, demanding he leave her apartment. In the recording, he could hear Malcolm telling Santina that she was his forever, and that he would kill her new lover if she didn't break up with him.

"I'm tired of your bullshit. You're a jealous jerk, and I need you and your friends to leave my apartment now. Your drugs and alcohol are all you have in life," shouted Santina, as the message continued.

The next part of the voicemail sounded like there was a struggle. Glasses shattered, there was more yelling and screaming, and then the voicemail cut off. To Walter, it sounded as though Santina left her voicemail running to capture as much of the conversation as possible. That night, Walter fell asleep amid a tangle of tears, regret and exhaustion.

In the middle of the night, Walter woke up screaming. Justice could hear him from his bedroom and burst into Walter's room to see what was going on. There in the bed, he saw his brother sweating profusely and crying.

"After you left, I listened to another voicemail she left. I had a nightmare I was in her apartment during the assault and I could hear her yelling out for me from the next room. She was begging me to help her and when I entered the bedroom, I saw her reaching out her hand, but the farther I reached out to save her, the greater the space between us grew.

"I felt so close to being there, but I was never close enough. I feel so vulnerable. I blame myself for not taking her ex-boyfriend's threat from last year more seriously. I saw the clues when I had to drag him out of the building, but figured he was a joker who didn't require any thought or attention.

"I thought I had this all figured out, but I couldn't protect her when she needed me. I feel so vulnerable. I saw myself spending the rest of my life with Santina and credit her for my maturity over the last few months. Prior to her, I would have never felt this way about a woman," Walter choked out.

Justice embraced his brother. "Do you remember what I mentioned in your ear that night in Baltimore? There was nothing you could have done to save Santina."

Walter understood his brother's words and agreed to go back to bed. Justice told Walter he was going to stay the night on his bedroom floor, and Walter agreed.

*****

The months following Santina's death were very difficult for Walter. There were many sleepless nights where he just lie in bed for hours thinking about Santina and life in general. The nights when he could fall asleep, he'd wake up in the middle of the night to cold sweats and panic. What Justice told him the night of Santina's murder reminded him of the comfort he felt when they were in Baltimore after the robbery.

There was something about those words that gave Walter comfort and reassurance that the future would be okay. But even with the advice from his brother, he still can't stop thinking about Santina.

Justice saw this and began brainstorming ideas to help with Walter's recovery. He finally came up with the perfect solution. "Let's take a trip. Let's book a plane ticket out of the country and just go."

"Where?"

"It doesn't matter; we just need to get away from all of this," Justice replied.

Walter nodded his consent.

Justice planned a trip for the two to separate themselves from reality and hit the reset button. The timing was perfect, because they were scheduled to attend a Fourth of July party on a rooftop in NYC that day, and were going to leave on vacation the following day.

*****

For the next four weeks, they visited Colombia, Costa Rica, Puerto Rico and the Dominican Republic. The clear water, white sand and aguardiente is just the therapy the brothers need.

For the sake of their peace and sanity, they turned off work phones and emails. For four weeks, they did nothing but sat poolside, hiked, swam, drank and partied with the locals. They spent about a week in each location, which was enough time to learn a little about the way of life in each country and immerse themselves in the culture.

At first, Walter thought it may be difficult to visit Colombia since Santina was Colombian. Instead, when he arrived, he realized that visiting her home country was a way of honoring her life. He never met her family, but when she was alive, she spoke a lot about Bogota, her family's home city. They spend a few days there and paid homage to her at a church in the middle of the city.

After returning from their vacation in August of that year, Walter told Justice that he was doing better and was ready to resume life.

"I'm happy to see you getting back to your normal self, because I am tired of you walking around this apartment looking like a 90's R&B music video," Justice joked.

The two brothers laughed and embraced with a handshake and hug.

"The summer traveling we did had a huge impact on me, and I think it was just the reset I needed. The past month has reminded me how hard life can be. How one deals with the hardships is what makes people strong. Our time together helped me realize life is short. If it hadn't been for our time together, I'd still be moping around and regretting certain decisions, both the ones I made and the ones I failed to make. The thing I have always found solace in was my work. It's always been the thing I could get lost in for hours because I am so good at it. I'm ready to focus my attention on work again.

The brothers agreed that they would make the next few months strong professionally and personally. Walter agreed to get back to work and in time start dating again. Justice told Walter his show resumed filming soon, so he, too, plans to get back to work.

*****

August was normally a dry and humid period in NYC. The brothers joked about how they went from the beaches of San Andres to the choking humidity of the Flatiron District.

Despite this change in scenery, they had no real complaints. The summers in NYC were typically much more active than the winters because of the rooftop openings and outdoor seating options in many restaurants. August also meant restaurant week was in full effect, which Walter looked forward to every year. As a foodie, this was his excuse to dine at as many restaurants in the city as possible, while taking advantage of their affordable prices.

"Since this is our first restaurant week in NYC, I want us to set a goal to dine at as many Michelin-star-rated restaurants as we can. I know you probably plan to take Ana to some of these restaurants, but I also want us to hit a few," Walter said to Justice.

"I agree. I think we need to enjoy the city before it gets cold out."

Their next few weeks are spent dining out, working out and drinking. A few of the restaurants they visited were Raymi, Inakaya, Tribeca Grill, Eleven Madison and Daniel.

Justice also made good on his plan to use this period as an opportunity to take Ana out on various impressive date nights. He made separate reservations for the two of them as Butter, Per Se and Ai Fiori.

CHAPTER 16:

BORN HEROES

Justice- September - October

The first phase of filming was shot in the cooler months so the director could capture scenes with the fall and winter. For four days every week between January and June of last year, Justice filmed for 14 hours a day. The days were long and his role is strenuous, but he loved it. He wanted to give the producers a reason to keep him on, and did so by showing his work ethic.

In his starring role, he knew he has an unspoken obligation to be on the set earlier and stay later than others. His aspiration for being one of the most-respected and sought-after actors in the world couldn't come without dedication, he reminded himself.

His desire to be the best also served as motivation to stay in shape and maintain his physical appearance. Manicures, pedicures, massages and facials are regular for Justice. He knew the importance of maintaining grooming standards and regularly scheduled appointments with his barber and massage therapist were key.

The current phase of filming was being shot in downtown Manhattan to capture the late summer/early fall scenery. Being that the focus was to capture a warmer period in the show, they were shooting in late August. Coming from a city like L.A. to a metropolis like New York City showed Justice the major differences in the lifestyle.

The weather alone was a determinant of people's moods. Just as Justice thought, the warmer months in Manhattan did not disappoint. The city was out and about and everyone was happy. It reminded him of Santa Monica beach. Justice loved flaunting his toned figure and took advantage of warmer days as an excuse to take off his shirt and show off the product of his gym work.

As if it couldn't get any better, the director told the cast and crew that they would receive extended time off for Labor Day weekend. When they returned, the plan was to shoot a music festival scene so the director invited friends and family to the set.

Justice didn't have enough friends in NYC to fill a music festival crowd, but knew he had at least two people who would be excited to join in the filming. He called Walter to tell him the exciting news, then calls Ana to come by. He also told Walter to invite some folks from Karot if he chose to.

*****

In the days following Labor Day, Walter, Ana and hundreds of other friends and family were on set as extras in the crowd of a music festival. Walter was proud to see how much progress his brother was having on the show and wanted to support him. Knowing Justice needed plenty of extras for the scene, Walter decided to bring Malia, Robert and ten of his other coworkers to the set.

While on set, Walter introduced his brother as the future face of the Academy Awards. Justice beamed with pride, thanked everyone for joining and encouraged everyone to watch the show when it debuts.

*****

One late October day, the cast and crew of the Netflix drama were wrapping up their filming when the cast heard screaming from the next block over. Because of the filming, there had been unusual noises all day, so they assumed it was nothing serious and continued filming.

They then heard another, louder scream coming from the same direction, but this time they saw a group of pedestrians fleeing down the street through their set. The group looked panicked, which caught the attention of the cast and crew.

"Cut! What the hell is going on?" yelled the director.

Justice followed the director's instructions and focused his attention on the group of pedestrians. He told himself something didn't seem right, but no one stopped to say anything, so he didn't quite know how to react.

Someone heard one of the pedestrians yell the word "bomb," so most of the cast and crew began running alongside the pedestrians. Something didn't seem right to Justice, who was still unconvinced he needed to follow the crowd. He grabbed one of the pedestrians and asked him what is going on.

The pedestrian seemed very worried and was crying hysterically. He didn't say anything. Justice released his grip on the man's shoulders and allowed him to keep running. He then turned his attention toward the commotion and saw people laid out on the concrete at the end of the block. He began running in that direction. He wanted to see what was going on, and knew he wouldn't get any answers from the people running past.

When he reached the end of the block, he noticed a few pedestrians lying in the middle of the street and on the sidewalk. They seemed like they had either collapsed or had been hit by something. It was then that he noticed a truck at the end of the sidewalk, driving away from the bodies on the pavement. It was obvious that the truck hit the bystanders and was turning around to hit others.

Justice quickly took in the scene and saw a young mother with her son desperately attempting to flee. The mother was having a difficult time running with her son, and the truck was now accelerating toward the pair. Justice knew they couldn't outrun the driver and, in that moment, decided he needed to do something.

Without thinking twice, he began running at the woman and her son. The driver accelerated faster when he saw Justice running across the street toward the pair. Unbeknownst to the mother, the driver had his sights on her and was now gunning for her and her son. As Justice and the driver made their way to the woman, the driver accidentally hit a trash can, which threw his acceleration off. Unfortunately, Justice also hit a similar hiccup while crossing the street, but continued toward the mother.

They both continued moving forward, and Justice beat the driver, reaching the mother in just enough time to knock her and her son out of the way. In his attempt to save them, Justice wrapped his arms around them and tackles them. They all went tumbling down the concrete pathway. His wrapped arms help protect the mother and her son from impact. They rolled down the sidewalk until coming to a sudden stop by hitting a bench.

Justice looked up to see that the truck had collided with a bus. As the driver exited the vehicle, the police arrived on the scene and were closing in on him. Justice then looked over the mother and asked if she and her son were okay.

"We're okay. You saved our lives," the young mother said, tearing up.

"Shhh...You're safe now."

"For a quick second, I thought it was over for us. My name is Moriah and this is my son, David. Why did you help us?" the mother asked.

"As weird as this may sound, I didn't choose to save you. I sort of felt like I was chosen to save you. I was down the block filming. When I heard the commotion, something made me run toward it. When I got wind of what was going on, I felt it was my responsibility to try to help you because you needed me," Justice replied.

Moriah began to cry harder. "You must be either incredibly brave or incredibly stupid to put yourself in danger like that."

"You were the one in danger, I was just in the right place at the right time. If that makes me brave or stupid, then I understand."

Moriah hugged Justice, thanking him profusely.

After their embrace, Justice saw blood on the mother's hands and asked if she was okay.

"I'm fine and David seems okay, too," she replied, examining her body. "Are you okay? It looks like the blood may be coming from you."

When she looked closer at the back of Justice's head, she noticed blood was running down from an open wound. He felt the back of his head and could touch the blood running down. He then felt himself getting dizzy and collapsed in the middle of the sidewalk. Moriah yelled for help, and fortunately the paramedics were already on the scene.

They rushed over to Justice, and Moriah explained there was an open wound on the back of his head. The paramedics looked at the wound then quickly loaded Justice into the ambulance and began to transport him to the hospital. Moriah and David chose to ride in the ambulance because they wanted to ensure Justice was okay.

"What happened to him?" asked the paramedic

"This man saved us from being run over by grabbing us and moving us out of the way. In the act of saving us, I think he might have hit his head on the sidewalk…or the bench. Why didn't he feel it?" inquired Moriah.

"From what it looks like, he may have been in shock from the ordeal. Because of the adrenaline, the injury may not have registered at first. It wasn't until he saw the blood that his brain began to associate the injury with the pain."

While in the ambulance, Justice began drifting in and out of consciousness.

"Please talk to him. We need to keep him awake and alert. We're not sure if he has a concussion. A trick we normally like to use is to ask open-ended questions. It may be wiser to just ask him yes or no questions since we're asking him not to speak during transport," the paramedic said.

Moriah found Justice's wallet and looked over the name and address on his ID. "Hi Justice, I'm Moriah. Do you remember me?" Justice nodded his head.

"Great. I'm glad to see you can understand me. So, you hit your head saving me. Do you remember that? Did you see the kind of truck the driver was driving? I think we're going to a hospital downtown. Do you know what day it is?" Moriah continued.

When they arrived at the hospital, nurses and doctors transported Justice to a room and began to examine his head in hopes of determining the extent of the injury.

From his hospital room, the nurse continued asking him a series of questions including his name, the date and if he knows what happened.

By now, Justice was able to speak and answered the questions.

"Yes. Today is Monday, October 23, 2017. I think I'm here because I hit my head while helping Moriah and David," Justice replied.

This was a good sign. The doctor came in to examine Justice and speak with Moriah. After further examination, the doctor determined Justice had a mild concussion and will need stitches and some rest to recover.

Justice asked for his phone so he can call his brother to let him know where he is. Moriah handed him his cell, which she picked up from the ground after their fall.

Justice called Walter. "Hey Walt, I'm in the hospital. I hit my head helping a woman. I'm okay, just need a few stitches, then I'll probably be heading home. The woman and her son came with me to the hospital, so I'm not alone."

Justice handed the phone to Moriah and said his brother wanted to speak with her. When she picked up, Walter thanked Moriah for bringing his brother to the hospital and for staying with him. He then asked her if Justice would be okay.

"The doctors believe he'll be fine. They're saying it's a mild concussion and he should be fine… Oh, you're welcome. I'm more than happy to stay with him," she replied, handing the phone back to Justice.

Justice asked his younger brother to come by the hospital when he was done with work, then hangs up.

"My brother's on his way. You and David don't have to stay. I'm sure you're probably exhausted from today. You can head home. I'll wait for Walter," Justice said.

"Thanks for your offer, Justice, but we aren't going anywhere. You were there for us, and we'll be here for you until your brother arrives. I'm going to go to the cafeteria in a few to get some food for David. What can I grab for you?"

"Nothing for me. I'm not hungry…but I have some things I want to write down. Do you see a pen and pad anywhere?"

She handed him the pen and pad from the table and left the room with her son.

A few hours passed since Justice arrived at the hospital. The doctors had stitched him up and put a bandage on his head. They also provided him with acetaminophen, which they told him should relive some of the pain.

Justice took the pain medication and felt himself getting tired, so he wrote down his thoughts. He didn't want to risk forgetting anything by the time his brother arrived. He placed the note on the counter next to the bed, and lays his head down to rest.

As they walked back from the cafeteria, Moriah and David saw the nurse and doctor running down the hall toward Justice's room. As she followed, she overheard the nurse tell the doctor the patient was seizing.

When they arrived at the room, the nurse closed the door in Moriah's face and asked her to wait outside. But before the door shut, she saw Justice's body jerking uncontrollably, and heard machines beeping.

From outside the room, she could hear the commotion. She also heard a defibrillator being used. Minutes later, a different doctor came out to speak with Moriah.

"Are you an immediate family member?" he asked.

"No, I'm just a friend. Is he okay?"

"Unfortunately, I can't say. I need to talk to a family member," the doctor said.

"His brother is on his way. I'll be wait in the waiting room for him."

Moriah walked to the waiting room with David and sat down. She told David the man from earlier was sick and she wants him to pray for him.

CHAPTER 17:

"LOVE, J."

Walter - September - October

It is now September 5, and Walter was heading to downtown Manhattan to help Justice with filming a few scenes. Last week, Justice invited Walter and his Karot colleagues to the set so they could help out with filming a music festival scene. When Walter told Robert a few others from Karot also agreed to support his cause. When he told Malia, she invited a few of her sorority sisters from Alpha Kappa Alpha who were based in Manhattan professionally. Walter even called X and Sheun, but neither were planning to be in NYC during the filming.

In reviewing his schedule for the month, Walter noticed he was scheduled to be in Chicago and Tampa for a seminar and Seattle for a roadshow.

September was looking like a busy month, and Walter welcomed his onus.

Outside of the Labor Day invitation, Walter hadn't seen his brother in some time because he had been staying at Ana's home. When he was not with Ana, Justice was filming. The trip they took this summer was the perfect way to jump back into their busy schedules.

Now that his mourning period was over, Walter found himself beginning to accept dates again and felt comfortable putting himself back on the market. Over the past few weeks he went on several dates, but similar to Brenna, he was unable to find a connection with any of the women he went out with. This caused him to dive deeper into his work, which resulted in him spending a lot of time in the office.

*****

One late October afternoon, Walter was working at the Karot office when he received a call from his brother. Walter listened as Justice explained how there had been an incident in downtown Manhattan and he helped save a woman who was almost run over by a lunatic. He said he sustained some minor injuries, but the doctors believed he would be okay. Walter almost didn't believe it until he turned on the television and saw the news. As he watched, he saw them talking about the terrorist attack. Walter then said he would contact Ana to see if she could meet him at the hospital. Justice replied by telling Walter that Ana was in Milan for the week, and that he would call her instead.

"Can I talk to the woman who brought you to the hospital?... Hi, I'm Walter, Justice's brother. I want to thank you from the bottom of my heart for bringing my brother to the hospital and staying with him. Will he be okay? ... Thank you. Can I speak with Justice again, please?" Walter asked.

After she handed the phone back to Justice, Walter listened as Justice told him not to worry.

A relieved Walter agreed to stop by the hospital when he got off work in a few hours. Walter tried to go back to work, but couldn't concentrate with Justice in the hospital. He rearranged his afternoon and canceled a few calls so he could leave work.

After fighting NYC traffic, which was only made worse because of the terrorist attack, Walter finally managed to get to the hospital a little after six. When he arrived, he made his way to the main desk where he saw a cute receptionist sitting.

"Good afternoon, I'm here to see Justice Benine. He was recently brought in to treat a minor head injury," Walter stated.

"Wow, Justice has been quite popular since he arrived," replied the receptionist.

Walter didn't understand the comment, but disregarded it when she handed him a sign-in clipboard. She asked Walter to please wait in the waiting room while she grabbed a nurse, and he obliges.

As he made his way to the waiting room, he noticed a few others who look like they were also injured during the attack. As he entered the waiting room, he quickly looked around, and thought he might recognize the mother he spoke with on the phone, but wasn't sure.

The mother he saw was staring vacantly, sitting next to her teenage son. The two of them made eye contact and exchanged smiles.

Unbeknownst to Walter, Moriah and David are actually sitting behind him in the waiting room.

As he began to get up to introduce himself to the mother and her teenage son, a doctor came out and called for Walter Benine. Walter responded, and began walking toward the back with the doctor.

Moriah recognized the name and swiftly focused her attention toward the doctor and Walter, but before she could react or introduce herself, they disappeared behind the door.

As they walked toward the room, the doctor informed Walter that there were some complications over the past few hours with Justice's recovery.

"The head injury your brother suffered was far worse than we originally assumed. He began bleeding internally because of his brain swelling. In an effort to monitor and save his brain functionality, we had to place him into a medically induced coma. If we hadn't done that, he would've died from seizing out and we wouldn't have been able to stop the bleeding," the doctor claimed.

A confused Walter looked at the doctor and replied, "That can't be true. I *literally* just spoke with him a few hours ago, and he sounded fine. He said it was just a mild concussion and that he was going to get some rest."

"Yes, that's what we originally believed, but while he was resting, he began to bleed through his stitches because of the swelling."

Walter, who was now in disbelief, arrived outside of Justice's room and asked the doctor and nurse for privacy while he visited his brother.

As Walter entered the room and was horrified at what he saw. The one person who has always been the strongest person he knows now lays in the hospital bed, helpless. His body looked lifeless and he was hooked up to machines that are monitoring his brain and heart activity. *He sounded so full of life on the phone. How can he be in a coma now?*

Walter tapped his older brother on the shoulder to let him know he was there, but doesn't receive a response or reaction. Walter had always believed in God because of his parents, but never considered himself a fully religious person.

He knew there was a higher being looking out for him and his brother, but always wondered to what extent. He had seen people at their absolute highest and at their lowest. Without assigning blame, Walter lowered his head, put his hands together and began to pray for his brother's health and speedy recovery.

When he was done with his prayer, he lifted his head and saw a letter with his name on it sitting on the counter beside his brother's bed. The note was written in Justice's handwriting, so Walter read it. The letter read:

1. *Finish filming (season 1)*
2. *Go on another trip with Walter*
3. *Get married*
4. *Ensure Moriah and David are okay*
5. *Mentor David*

Hey Bro,

Above are a few of my to-do's once I get out of this hospital. It's crazy what almost dying can do to a person. Today's terrorist attack reminded me of two things. First, the world is the scary place Mom and Dad told us about. It's filled with terrible people who want to see the positive aspects of life go up in flames. To think, when Mom and Dad told us that when we were kids, I didn't fully grasp the idea until now. Without any scientific backing, I believe some people just want to destroy anything good.

The second thing I was reminded of is the fact that I am not and will never be one of those people. I can never allow myself to stand by and let the world burn when there is so much beauty in it. Today was an example of the realities of both. The mother and child I helped reminded me that I will always put myself in a position to stop the world from burning. I've probably never told you this, but I think I get that from you.

Crazy thing about today's situation is before reacting, I thought to myself, "What would Walter do in this situation?" I believe if you were in the same situation, you would have reacted the same way. That was part of the reason I ran "toward the flames" instead of "away from the fire."

Even if I've never said it, you are an inspiration to me, baby bro. Somewhere between wrapping up my filming and getting married, we need to take another trip like we did this past summer. It was honestly one of the best experiences in my life! I also plan to mentor the kid I saved. I am realizing that our purpose in this world is to influence young people like him for the better. I had some friends his age in L.A., and this kid reminds me so much of them.

Another reason I plan to mentor the kid is so he can help us prove why it's important for reason number two to always outweigh reason one. I'm going to get some rest now, but when I wake, hopefully you're here so we can get me out of this hospital.

Love,

J.

As Walter wrapped up reading the letter, he began to tear up because he was hearing all of this in a letter instead of in his brother's voice. The nurse who was treating Justice came in to see Walter.

She introduced herself and told him that Justice was a hero and that they were doing everything they could for him. She said that the woman and child who he saved are outside in the waiting room and would like to meet him. Walter agreed, so the nurse brought Moriah into the room. They embraced and, for about 10 minutes, cried silently on each other's shoulders.

"Neither me nor my child would be here if it weren't for your brother. He came out of nowhere and saved us from being run over. He is a hero, and I am praying for him," Moriah choked out.

"I'm not surprised. As far back as I can remember, that was always the kind of person Justice was. Our parents once told us that I was the one who cared about protecting people, but I think I got it from him. He always looked out for me, even when I didn't realize it. He left a note on the counter and there were two points in the note about you and your son. Justice said he wants to make sure you and your son are okay, and he'd like to mentor David.

Walter turned his attention to the nurse, and asked what he can do for Justice now.

"Unfortunately, only time will tell if he will recover from the swollen brain. At this point, we just need to give him rest and hope for the best."

Walter exchanged contact information with Moriah and advised her to go home and get some rest. It was well after visiting hours, but he said he'd like to wait with his brother. Moriah and Walter hugged, and she left the hospital.

Walter spent most of the next seven days in the room with Justice. Justice didn't show any change in condition, which the nurse said could be a good thing because it meant he hadn't gotten worse.

Walter didn't want to leave his brother's side, so he took time off from work. He also informed his various volunteering organizations that he was taking some time away to deal with a personal matter.

On day eight, the doctor came in to speak with Walter, again informing him that there was no change in Justice's condition. This time, though, he added that he was worried there might not be any further improvement. He told Walter that he wanted to present him with all of his options because his brothers hospital bill was growing, and he felt the need to make Walter aware. He mentioned that in the past, he had never seen a patient recover from this kind of head injury. He had hoped Justice would be different, but based on the past few days, he did not feel he will.

"I disagree. My brother is a fighter, and I'm sure you're wrong. He used to be a football star. He fought back from injuries far worse than this," claimed Walter.

"I'm sorry, sir. I'm sure you're tired and this is the last thing you want to hear, but I need to tell you that we may only be delaying the inevitable here. Have you considered what comes next in regard to taking him off life support? It may be the only outcome."

"You're wrong! What do you even know? I understand you want to close this patient file and hit the golf course, but NO. Do what they pay you to do and fix my brother!" Walter shouted.

The doctor saw that Walter's exhaustion, fear and anxiety were making him very emotional. He recommended Walter take some time out of the hospital and go get some rest.

He mentioned that they will continue to monitor Justice for the next few days and call him with any changes. Walter was hesitant at first, but reluctantly agreed because he also believed he should ensure his emotional well-being was not affected by his worry for Justice. He told the doctor he was headed home for the day and would return in two days after he got some rest.

"I'll see you in two days," the doctor agreed.

*****

While riding the train home, Walter began sweating profusely and breathing rapidly. He asked for a seat on the E Train to compose himself, a request other commuters obliged. They saw him having a panic attack, and moved out of the way in fear for Walter losing himself. Once he sat down, Walter dropped his head and began thinking about everything going on in his life. In addition to what the doctor stated about Justice, Walter again thought about losing Santina and thought to himself, *why is this happening to me?*

That question prompted Walter to once again think back to what the old man told him about the emptiness and regret in his face. With his head still lowered, he exhaled his breath and slapped his forehead.

The emptiness the old man saw in my face might have been because he foresaw that I was going to lose Santina and Justice. Wait, that sounds stupid. He didn't seem supernatural.

After a few moments, Walter then lifted his head and put both hands on his head as if he made a discovery.

How could I be so stupid? The old man said there was an emptiness in my face. Maybe what he saw was in the person I believed I needed to be.

Walter then rehashed a the conversation he had with Santina, and realized he answered his own question during that conversation.

After the 9/11 attack I felt vulnerable and scared. After the Baltimore robbery, I needed to be the provider and protector my mom and dad said I was to never feel that vulnerability again. Not giving up my possessions that day was my subconscious attempting to protect my friends and I. Sadly, I could not stop them from being robbed, and Justice ended up coming to protect us. Maybe this emptiness I have been feeling is my need to return the favor and protect Justice.

Justice getting injured helped Walter arrive at this breakthrough. He realized that his subconscious felt in debt to Justice for protecting him, and regret for being the cause of their separation as teens.

Walter shook his head to clear it, and went over the doctor's comments. He considered what life would be like without Justice. They had been apart for so long, had just gotten back together and now Justice was being taken from him again. After thinking about it, he began to ask himself why he was cursed. He thought about all the remarkable initiatives and volunteering that he committed to. *How could this be how my story goes?* he asked himself.

As the E pulled up to the next stop, he ran off the train and toward the street for some air. He felt as though he was being suffocated, and needed air to help him think.

After spending a few minutes catching his breath, he decided to numb his pain. He stopped by a wine and liquor store and picked up a bottle of Blanton Bourbon. As he stood in line, he looked at the bottle convinced himself the alcohol will help to numb the pain he felt.

When he left the liquor store, he quickly removed the cap and took a sip. As the warm liquor coated his throat, he realized that being numb wasn't all he needed. He believed he was lost and needed guidance.

Walter decided that the best place to seek guidance was from his parents, because they have always provided him with insight on tough life decisions. He pulled out his phone, entered the destination into his Uber app and waited for a driver to accept the ride and pick him up.

When the driver showed up, Walter told him he was going to visit his parents. The driver looked at the location, then back at Walter to verbally confirm it. When Walter nodded, and the car slowly eased back into traffic.

They pulled up to the location in upstate New York. The driver, noticing they were at a cemetery, asked Walter if everything was okay. Walter replied that he was okay. He mentioned his parents had passed a few years back and he was going to visit their graves. Walter then said thank you, and got out of the vehicle.

After tipping the driver and rating him five stars on the app, Walter decided to turn off his phone because he wanted to be alone.

CHAPTER 18:

"HOW HAVE I WRONGED YOU?"

Walter

While walking toward his parents' burial site, Walter was hit with an immense amount of sadness and regret.

Like the feelings he felt when Santina died, his doubt of himself began to overwhelm him and his depression resurfaced. In a painful cry for help, Walter screamed, "How have I wronged you?" looking to the sky as if he were speaking to God.

As he took another sip of his bourbon, he found himself beginning to have another panic attack. Walters legs went numb, his vision blurred and he dropped to his knees.

As tears ran down his face, he put his hands over his eyes and began sobbing. While on the ground, he saw a rope and shovel beside him, and grabbed them both.

He again asked, "How I have wronged you?" this time following it up with, "How much more you do you want from me?"

He attempted to compose himself by wiping his eyes, then looked around. He saw that he was kneeling beside an empty grave located under a tree. He was worn and fatigued. Fortunately for him, he fell in the shadow of the huge tree and out of the hot sun.

As tears continued to slowly run down his face, Walter began to wallow in his loneliness and the idea he believed he was being punished. When he looked down again, he told himself the empty grave in front of him looked as though it was outfitted for him.

"How have I wronged you? I don't understand why I've been forsaken," Walter remarked in a desperate plea for help.

Something happened just then which came as a shock to Walter. He felt a hand on his shoulder and heard the voice of what sounded like an elderly man. In a soft, harmonious tone, the elderly man told Walter that he wasn't asking the right questions.

"The answers you seek will not come from the questions you are asking. The answers you need will come from the questions you are *failing* to ask," the old man said.

A shocked Walter finds control of himself again and stumbled backward from surprise. When he got up and wiped his eyes, he indeed saw an elderly man dressed in a gravedigger's uniform standing beside him at the empty grave.

The digger was wearing dirt-stained overalls and has a shovel in one hand and a knapsack on his back. He has a light coat of facial hair with wavy salt-and-pepper hair on his head. He looked at Walter and once again told him that he was asking the wrong questions.

Walter told the gravedigger he didn't want any company; he preferred to be alone.

"What purpose will that serve?" the man asked.

Now frustrated, Walter replied in a sarcastic tone, demanding that, "The purpose of being alone is so I don't have to answer dumb questions from old men who don't make any sense, so leave me alone." Walter subconsciously gritted his teeth. "I don't want to talk about it."

"Well, it seems like you don't want to talk about anything. Are you telling me you came to the graveyard to leave the same way you came in? I find that hard to believe, and think you're searching for something. I can tell that what you are searching for is not obvious to you, so you feel lost. This isn't you, and if peace is what you seek, you won't find it where you're looking."

Walter stubbornly ignored him, looking down at the grave.

"You have been broken. But that rope will not repair your broken pieces," explained the gravedigger.

As he looked down, Walter noticed that in his frustration and anger, he subconsciously created a noose with the rope in his hands. He instantly dropped the rope and grabbed his bottle instead.

"You will not find the peace you seek in the bottom of a bottle, the bottom of that grave or at the end of the rope," the old man offered. "You believe your truth is in the perfect image of yourself, but I want to help you see that it is the times we realize our imperfections that will give you the absolution you seek."

"Listen old man, you don't even know me. You talk about imperfections, but you're just a gravedigger."

"I may be 'just a gravedigger,' but I know more about you than you think, young man. I know that you have a pure heart and that you have a lot more to contribute to the world. Your potential is just being realized, and the fact that you've been hurt recently should not dissuade you from the good you're doing in the world," replied the old man.

Walter, who was now a quarter of the bottle in, looked at the gravedigger. "What do you know of my potential? I've committed myself to being the best at my craft. For years, I've sacrificed everything to achieve enough success to protect those around me. As much as it has been about me, it has also been about those whom I wanted to empower and enlighten. My fundraising and volunteerism have always held a piece of my heart, but my 70-plus-hour work weeks have been the true cost of my success.

"I've also made life all about my commitment to children. What will they think of me now? How am I supposed to empower and protect them when I can't even protect those closest to me? I've done everything right, and the only thing I've received in return is to lose the love of my life and my brother in the same year. I give up. What's the point of trying anymore? I'd rather make this part easy and give up."

The old man stared at Walter with all the compassion he could muster. "Thank you for sharing your truths, young man. That was an honest moment you shared with me, and I am very grateful for you opening up. From what I can see, you are indeed hurting, which is factoring into you asking the wrong question.

"You are asking 'how have I wronged you,' but do you not understand what that means? That statement implies that your current situation is a result of some sort of punishment bestowed upon you. I'm here to tell you that you are wrong," stated the old man.

Walter stared at the gravedigger with a confused look. "What is the right question, old man?"

"The thing about it being the right question is that it must come from you," replied the gravedigger. "Every person's truth is their own to discover, and only you can realize your truth.

"I'm only here to help guide you to it, but I can't be the one to discover it for you. Every decision you have ever made has led to this moment in time. Whether you were working 100-hour weeks or volunteering your time, those decisions have factored into this moment.

"I'd like to apologize for the loss of your girlfriend. It sounds like she really meant a lot to you. Despite what you may believe, your actions did not cause her death. I also lost someone very close to me, and like you, it destroyed me. I'm not here with you because I gave up. Instead, I'm here because I overcame that challenging time in my life and think you can, too. Your actions have been an important determinant in the lives of many. It's provided those in need with better living conditions, a stable supply of food, running electricity and educational opportunities. There is still a lot for you to do, and the grave is the last place for you to do it.

"I can tell the reason you've done these things is not because you've felt obligated, but more because you understand your position. You approach life with a clean heart, and this results in the purest intentions.

"You don't even know me, old man. What makes you think any of that is true?" asked Walter.

"Why are we here?" the old man replied.

Walter thought back to the series of events that led to their meeting in the graveyard.

Despite the well-thought-out speech Walter was preparing in his head, he was unable to articulate the words to answer the old man's question.

With a confused look on his face, Walter told the old man that he did not know why they were there, and also, he did not need a lecture.

"I prefer to be alone, and would like to ask you to leave, old man," demanded Walter.

"But I am really beginning to enjoy our conversation and would prefer to stick around." the old man said, folding his hands in front of him. "I'm not going to make any assumptions, but if you came to this cemetery to do what I think you came to do, you'd be ripping the world off. You would be robbing the world of your ideas, creativity, love, compassion, innovation, drive, creativity, and best of all, your empathy."

"I don't know what to think any more. I always feel like I'm doing well when it seems like something happens to brings me ten steps back. My girlfriend dying crushed me, but I picked up the pieces and continued with life. If not for my brother, I'd still be in pain. Now my brother is brain dead, and I once again am left questioning why I do it. With all the money, power, and success that I've achieved over the past few years, it still wasn't enough," Walter sputtered.

"Do you believe that the money, the power or the success defines you?"

"No. I *know* it doesn't, but it definitely motivates me and helps drive many of my decisions," replied Walter.

"Okay, that's fair. Now imagine your life without an excess of money, power to control the things that happen in your life, or a successful career. Who would you be?"

Walter took a moment to consider the question and was unable to answer at first. "I… I would just be Walter Benine."

"But who is Walter Benine?" the old man asked.

"I don't know, man. I'm just me."

"I think you believe you know who you are, but also believe you should be someone else. You live out your purpose every day, but for some reason think it is the smallest part of who you are. Your value to this world goes way beyond the people you care about or your net worth," claimed the old man

"I don't care about my purpose, net worth or what the world thinks of me. The only person I'm worried about is lying in a hospital bed teetering on the edge of life and death. He's supposed to be superman."

The gravedigger shook his head slowly in disagreement. "The reason your brother made the decision to save that woman instead of running away with the others was because of the example you set. Outside of firefighters and police officers, there aren't many other people who would risk their life for another person, especially a complete stranger. In the many years I've walked this earth, I think I can comfortably say I've met no more than ten people who I believe will risk their life for someone else without being told to or having some sort of incentive. I don't know him, but I believe Justice may be the eleventh on my list."

After that, the gravedigger, turned around and began to walk away.

In thinking about their conversation, Walter knew he hadn't mentioned Justice's name or spoke about the event during which he saved Moriah. He knew this because the entire time they spoke, he only spoke about himself or his brother in third person.

Walter was shocked the gravedigger knew his brother's name and about him saving Moriah and her son. He ran after the gravedigger and stopped him. "How do you know about my brother?"

"I know about what happened with Justice because I am supposed to know. The reason we're both at this graveyard talking is because we need each other. In our overlapping story, both of us were meant to be at the same place at the same time because one of us seeks deliverance and the other seeks redemption.

"My job as a gravedigger is nothing more than my position. Outside of that, my purpose is to be here for you, because I believe you need me. Trust me when I say that I understand my purpose is greater than digging homes for the deceased.

"I knew three other great individuals who remind me of you and Justice. They were not great because of how they looked, how much money they had or where they came from. The thing that made them great was what was in their hearts and how they were using it to change the world," claimed the old man.

Walter was now extremely interested in what was being said as he tried to wrap his head around his current situation. While doing so, he stared intently at the gravedigger, and asked who the three individuals were.

"I'll share their stories, because I believe you need to hear them. At the conclusion, if they have no effect on you, I'll walk away, leave you be and you will never have to see me again," promised the old man.

He jokingly told Walter that the only other caveat is that Walter must share the bourbon during story time to keep him speaking. A less depressed and more interested Walter agreed because he knew he wasn't going anywhere and was still interested in learning about how the gravedigger knew about Justice.

The gravedigger dug into his knapsack, grabbed two empty plastic cups and handed them to Walter.

Walter poured them each a generous portion and told the gravedigger that if the stories bored him, he would cut off the bourbon supply and send him packing.

The gravedigger chuckled his agreement, cleared his throat and started from the beginning.

PART VI
WHO WILL SAVE ME FROM MYSELF?

CHAPTER 19:

THE JOVIAL GIANT

Eugene Garry

In 2008, the United States of America went through the Great Recession, which caused the worst GDP decline since the 1980's. Jobs were lost, homes were taken and families were destroyed.

Despite the downturn, Eugene Garry was one of the people who was not affected by any of these things. Fortunately, because of his work ethic and production, Eugene made it through the recession unscathed and was now happily taking advantage of the new wave of technology coming into the industry in 2016. He was a Wall Street broker of fifteen years by day and a superdad by night.

Despite his high-paying job, Eugene did not have many valuables or material items. To him, the greatest value in his life was the smile he could put on his two children's faces. Eugene was happily married to his college sweetheart, who also pursued a career in banking until the two of them decided it would be best if she tended to the children while he continued working to support the family. One of his two daughters had muscular dystrophy, so someone needed to be there to care for her at most times. The arrangement was perfect, and everything was taken care of. Eugene continued working as a Wall Street day trader to manage the family finances, health coverage and overall lifestyle, and his wife focused on the children's health, education, extracurricular activities and the family's overall involvement in the community.

They loved their lifestyle and were excited for what the future entailed. Eugene was one of the few tenured employees on Wall Street who made it out of the recession unscathed.

Since he began working on Wall Street, Eugene was determined to be the best. Not just for himself, but for everyone who would gain opportunities in the future because of the precedents he set. He knew the challenges that others who looked like him faced and understood his positioning in this world was to be more than just a broker.

He committed himself to removing the ceilings that people create for themselves due to race, gender or sexual orientation. His approach was that people were all here for a purpose, and everyone played a part in this melting pot of the world.

For that reason, Eugene made it a point to say "hi" and acknowledge as many people as possible with eye contact and a greeting. Whether you were the CEO or the summer intern, you were a person, and Eugene wanted you to know that. Before Eugene graduated from college, one of his favorite professors told him that the price of doing something nice for someone was the same as the price of doing something bad to someone. The main difference is doing something bad to someone usually came with an additional cost.

Unlike many of his colleagues, Eugene did not receive a diploma from a top ten accredited business school. His education was achieved at a public university in the middle of New Jersey where a career path in education was standard. Fortunately for him, his degree was enough to land him his dream job. He understood this and knew there was a greater meaning behind his continued success in corporate America.

Despite the difference in schooling, the only thing that mattered in the financial jungle was who was the hungriest and produced. Eugene knew he was the hungriest, and his colleagues saw it. Some admired his vigor and saw it as a form of strength for the brokerage, while others saw it as a direct barrier to them being considered the best.

Unlike many of the other traders in the office, Eugene loved mentoring the new hires and interns because he knew the overall success of the brokerage was determined by the lowest hanging fruit. Sadly, not everyone in the brokerage viewed colleagues in the same manner.

Eugene believed that the difference between those who advanced quickly and those who remained stagnant was the concept of "this or that," versus "both." Eugene viewed his contribution as a fraction of the firm's overall success and loved seeing the greater team win. He was a firm believer in the concept of "both."

Two brokers viewed Eugene as a direct competitor to their success. Justin and Daniel were looking to make a name for themselves in the industry and figured they'd make their name by taking down Goliath. They were three years removed from New York University and believed they were the hottest thing in the future of banking.

Immediately after their first full year with the brokerage, the brokers began to disassociate themselves from the others. They began to regularly challenge the feedback of others, disregard group initiatives and exclude themselves from team outings.

Despite those factors, the reason the two brokers were so successful in their roles was because they had very strong production numbers, which made others look past the other factors. Fortunately for them, the only thing that mattered to senior leadership was production. Often, the pair received tacit approval for their actions because others were afraid to act or speak on the treatment. Eugene was not one of those others.

Eugene was one of the few employees who called the pair out for their lack of team building and poor attitude toward the success of others. Because he helped mentor them when they first arrived to the firm a few years prior, Eugene believed he still had a mentor/mentee relationship. Eugene was mistaken, though, and over the next few months, he became the target of their treatment.

To undermine his credibility, the brokers regularly challenged everything Eugene did and said. They saw Eugene and others like him as dead weight that was holding them back. Unlike a few other seasoned colleagues, Eugene did not take it personally, and even took a liking to the competition.

To keep up, he worked to ensure he did not cut any corners and ensure his production was as close to perfect as possible. He looked at the competition as an opportunity for everyone to push each other to their highest performance levels.

To Eugene, the competition began and ended with the trades in the financial jungle, but to the young traders, the competition never ended. It often spilled outside of the trades.

To them, Eugene was an old-timer who was past his expiration date and did not fit with the new wave of millennials taking over the industry. They were determined to not only outperform him at every level, but make his life miserable in general.

There was one instance where Eugene walked into the kitchen and noticed the lunch his wife had prepared for him had been replaced by a brown bag of warm feces. This hurt Eugene and surprised him. He couldn't imagine anyone doing such a thing. And although he was disappointed by the malicious practical joke, he did not let it break him.

He knew he would probably never know who performed the disgusting act, so instead of putting time into finding out who wronged him, Eugene bought lunch that day and exerted his energy on the trading floor. That day ended up being one of his strongest days of production.

Despite the regular animus he received from Daniel and Justin, Eugene knew his success was much larger than himself. Eugene knew the treatment did not affect him, but saw the results of how it was beginning to affect others, so he acted.

When he saw colleagues who were hurt by the actions of the two traders, he reminded them that they must remember that when they signed their employment contract they were only promised a paycheck. They were never promised kindness, fairness or unity. He let them know he viewed the actions of the young traders as competition, which in turn allowed him to continue to do his best work.

One day he decided to bring the issue to his boss' attention in hopes that his boss would speak with the younger men's supervisor. Sadly, his boss was also aware of their production numbers and decided not to speak with their supervisor because he believed Eugene was being overly sensitive. His boss was wrong, and Eugene was one of the folks who did not allow the treatment to hurt him. Allowing them to get in his head was not an option. He would not let anything stop him from feeding his children.

One afternoon, Eugene's boss called him into the office to tell him the brokerage was experiencing some severe hardships due to the climate of the country and unfortunately, his job was being sent overseas. Immediately after the news was shared, three security guards soundlessly entered and stood in the back of the room. Eugene did not understand. He was crushing his numbers on a weekly basis and was regularly recognized for being one of the highest performers in the brokerage.

How could they disregard my tenure and performance? Eugene thought to himself. *Not only have I given this company the last fifteen years of my life, but my wife has sacrificed her own career so I could focus on mine.* He expressed his confusion with his manager, and asked for clarification on what factored into this decision.

"Your production has been spectacular, but the job is no longer available, Eugene," replied his manager.

In that moment, Eugene understood how real the situation was and that they were planning for him to not return to the office the next day. Various emotions began to come over Eugene as he tried to find the next words to say. He had many questions, but for some reason could not bring himself to ask them.

When he finally mustered up the words, he asked, "Where is Ashton Kutcher with the camera?"

"I'm sorry, Eugene. You're not being punk'd. This is a real situation we're in."

His embarrassment finally made its way to his face, so Eugene's manager asked if he understood the difficult situation the firm was in and hoped the working relationship could end on positive terms.

Without answering, Eugene turned around and walked out of the room. He stopped at his desk to collect the picture of his wife and kids, and then left the building.

As he drove home, Eugene's disappointment and embarrassment turned into anger. He refused to believe he was at the top of the chopping block during this round of layoffs. Eugene believed the explanation provided to him was complete bullshit, and he was entitled to the truth.

How could he tell his wife and kids that he lost his job because the brokerage decided it was best to send the role he's been doing for years, overseas? He decided to turn the car around, drive back to the office and demand answers.

Fortunately, Eugene had walked out before he could sign his termination papers, so his security badge still had access to the building. As he entered the parking garage, he noticed a building alarm going off.

When he asked the security guard what was going on, the security guard mentioned there was a physical altercation on the 8th floor and the building security team was tending to that call. This security guard somehow knew all the gossip and happenings of the building even before they were reported. On most days when he could, Eugene stopped by his booth and chatted with him for a few minutes before heading upstairs for work.

On this afternoon, Eugene didn't have time to chat with the guard. Instead, he made his way back upstairs and stormed into his manager's office to demand answers. The two young traders noticed Eugene enter the floor with exasperation and watched him walk into his manager's office. The pair heard Eugene was let go, so they sensed his energy was attributed to his termination.

Eugene immediately demanded answers from his manager. "Was my tenure with the brokerage even considered? I've mentored so many of the new traders and even continue to support them in their development over the years. How could my contributions over the year be so minuscule to this decision?" Eugene asked.

In that moment, Eugene's anger and voice began to raise. He felt his manager didn't have the answers to the questions because truthfully, there was no justification behind the termination.

"Eugene, we didn't want to embarrass you, but another factor toward the decision was the fact that there was some evidence shared about your work being completed by others. After a full investigation, it was determined that you were not producing results like others were," claimed his manager.

Eugene stared at his managed with a confused look. He refused to believe that answer and given his tenure and contributions, he demanded a better explanation.

"Well, the investigation proved that a few of your numbers were falsified," claimed the manager.

"What is the source of these claims and what kind of investigation was completed? I know this is a misdirection from the truth, and I refuse to believe I am not producing."

"There are a few brokers who said you've been unloading your work on them, which in turn made it difficult for them to produce a higher quality of work. They claimed that your high production rates were due to their efforts."

At that moment, Justin and Daniel entered the room and ask the manager if everything was okay.

"What is going on? Why are they here?" Eugene asked his boss. "Oh, this is all beginning to make sense now. This is just a ploy to undervalue me and my true work. My termination was somehow orchestrated, and I now understand who the 'few brokers' are." Eugene then focused his attention on the young traders. "Please leave the room so I can continue my conversation with my manager. The two of you have no reason to be here."

They sensed the tension in the room and told him they preferred to stay.

Eugene again asked the manager why they were in the room, but his manager steps back towards his desk because he was attempting to contact building security.

Unfortunately, due to the situation on the 8th floor, there were no security guards available to pick up the manager's call.

Eugene again asked Justin and Daniel to leave the room, but they ignored his request.

"We heard you were terminated. You really should just leave, Eugene. This doesn't have to be hard, and you should leave before you embarrass yourself," Daniel's face was filled with hatred.

The two traders were now beginning to feel anger toward a resistant Eugene and the manager who was still on the phone attempting to get help from security.

In their frustration, the traders approached Eugene to attempt to forcibly remove him from the room. Eugene resisted, stating he was waiting for an explanation from his manager.

As the traders attempted to wrestle Eugene out of the room, he tripped on the carpet and landed on his chest. Wrapping their arms around his arms and neck, the two traders tightened their grip to gain control of the resisting father of two.

With an exasperated breath, Eugene began to yell, "I can't breathe, I can't breathe, I can't breathe," until he couldn't yell any longer.

Despite his silence, the young traders did not relax their hold until the manager jumped off the phone and forcibly removed them from Eugene's lifeless body.

"What have you done?" the manager asked. He began yelling Eugene's name to his still body, but there was no reply. In that moment, the young traders realize what they'd done.

Moments later, the security guard from the parking garage entered the office and saw Eugene lying on the floor. He asked the manager what happened and was informed that Eugene was not breathing. The security guard attempted CPR on Eugene.

"Call 911! He isn't breathing," demanded the security guard.

After 10 minutes of CPR he stopped, dropped his head, and began tearing up. He then stood up, looked at the two brokers and the manager and said, "What have you done?"

CHAPTER 20:

THE EARLIEST BIRD IN BATON ROUGE

Peter Castile

At five o'clock in the morning, the alarm rang which signaled the start of the day for Peter Castile. As attractive as the snooze button seemed in that moment, he knew that the instant gratification of an extra ten minutes would be short-lived by the thought of his workload for the day.

Every second counted, and Peter was ready to add them up. Peter prided himself on being the earliest bird in Baton Rouge and believed that the quote, "the money doesn't sleep," was a direct influence on him. When others were heading home from a night of partying, he was getting up to start his day. Peter believed where there was commitment, attention and will, there would be results and satisfaction.

Unfortunately for Peter, he was the only person in his two-bedroom apartment who needed to wake up before the roosters began crowing, which made every morning that much more difficult than the previous. He loved waking up to the warm embrace of his long-time girlfriend, Ramona, who did not have to be into work until 9 a.m.

Unlike Ramona's job as a paralegal, Peter's job as a cafeteria cook required him to be at the school by 6 o'clock to begin prepping meals for his students. On paper, Peter knew he was a cook by trade. In his heart, he believed his true purpose was to be an educator of life and an example to the students through any means he could.

Unfortunately, due to some hardships early in his life, Peter did not have the funds and resources to finish his bachelor's degree in education. This resulted in Peter dropping out his junior year of college. Fortunately for Peter, after he left school, he secured a job at the elementary school he attended as a child.

In his heart, Peter knew he didn't need a college diploma to tell him that he could show young men how to treat a woman and show young women how to demand respect from the world. His passion was what kept him going, and he was determined to help as many adolescents as he could. On the surface was his apron and spatula but inside, Peter believed his true possibilities were endless.

While turning over to wish Ramona good morning with a kiss, he was instead greeted by her 6-year-old daughter, Annalise, who had slept with them after having a nightmare. Although Annalise occasionally had nightmares, she still loved watching films right before bed. For her, the late movies were gateways into her dreams. Peter preferred nonfiction books or biographies to films before bed. He wanted the last thing on his mind to be something he could share with the world the following day.

Peter loved the relationship he shared with Ramona and Annalise, and cherished the bond they shared over movies. He often found himself staying up late to read after the two of them fell asleep. He also used films as a great opportunity to connect with Annalise.

Since meeting Ramona three years earlier, Peter was proud of the progress he made as a man and as a positive male figure in Annalise's life. When Annalise slept in the bed with them, it often meant tighter sleeping quarters, which usually meant comfort was sacrificed. Instead of complaining about the limited space, Peter preferred the snuggles that came with the tight quarters. He was especially a fan of this in the winter.

As he made his way out of bed one morning, Peter was suddenly hit with fatigue. He had slept only five hours and was exhausted from pulling a double shift at his part-time job the night prior. To Peter, the fatigue was no excuse to "snooze his goals" and not give Ramona and Annalise the life they deserved. He knew he could take advantage of the moment when others would choose to sleep for another fifteen minutes.

He viewed those fifteen minutes as the only advantage he would receive in this world, so he had to take advantage. His success would come from his dedication to working harder than others.

Peter was also saving money in hopes of opening a resource center in his hometown for children who needed a safe space. Rather than resorting to street life, Peter wanted to build a space that children could feel was "a better option." Too many people Peter knew and grew up with fell victim to life on the streets in Louisiana because they did not feel they had another option. Most of the kids resorted to lives of theft or violence because they were sold on the street life. Most could not go home because their home situation was worse than it was in the streets. Peter was committed to doing what he could to change their futures.

When Peter was not feeding the appetites and minds of the students, he worked part-time as a waiter in the local diner. On most weekdays, Peter would leave the school by 2:30 p.m. and head straight to the diner to start his 4-hour shift. This day was no different, and Peter knew his morning coffee would help jump-start his body.

Peter's morning routine consisted of purchasing three coffees from Seymour's Coffee Shop around the corner from the school. His go-to was a medium French vanilla coffee with three sugars.

Peter had two close friends at work who were part of the reason he looked forward to the long days. They were the other cook, Ms. Mary, and the janitor, Obie. Peter always picked up two small black coffees with no milk, no sugar for his colleagues. The three of them had a great working relationship, and together their energy helped jump-start the busy mornings full of arrivals from teachers and students. They were an important reason for Peter's workplace happiness.

The three employees regularly set the tone before the rest of the kitchen and janitorial staff arrived around 7 a.m. Generally, the cooks liked to have breakfast ready by 7:20 a.m. so they could assist the teachers by serving as greeters for the 7:30 a.m. opening bell.

One April morning as the students began to flood the cafeteria, Peter and his two colleagues took their positions. Today was Thursday, which meant breakfast sandwiches, yogurt and orange juice.

Thursdays were generally a lighter breakfast, so while others took advantage of the lighter service, the janitor liked to jump behind the breakfast counter to assist with service.

Peter preferred to be on the cafeteria floor with the students and teachers on these lighter days. The first period bell was scheduled to ring at 7:45 a.m. every day, so Peter took advantage to make sure he spoke with as many people as possible. He loved talking to the students and teachers about world news, economics and what he was reading. He saw it as an opportunity to learn while teaching.

On this particular Thursday morning, Peter was speaking with the students about the chapter he read from the newly republished *Dreams From My Father*, which detailed the point in his life when President Barack Obama reconnected with his family on his father's side. Peter did not know his father growing up, so he connected with this section of the book the most.

Peter's colleagues admired the fact that he wasn't afraid to step out of his shell and put himself out there. His colleagues were a bit more reclusive, and feared being looked down upon because of their jobs. They believed they were viewed as "the help," and no one respected them as educated individuals. Most of his colleagues accepted that, which caused them to have little care for details or for doing more than was required in their job duties. Like the lack of a college degree, Peter did not see this as a barrier like his colleagues did.

Instead, he considered this an opportunity to remove the idea that "the help" was uneducated and boring. He believed he had a greater responsibility and knew he would fulfill it whether he was the school principal or the groundskeeper.

As the breakfast service concluded, the students began to make their way to their first period classes. Before assisting with the morning cleanup, Peter called Ramona to make sure she was awake and getting Annalise ready for school. Ramona mentioned that Annalise was already ready for school and they were about to leave the house shortly. Peter told Ramona he loved her and reminded her that she was a great mother and girlfriend. Ramona let Peter know that he received a voice message from the bank. She didn't hear any details, just that they wanted Peter to call them back.

As Peter continued with his morning duties, he checked his email and noticed a message from the bank stating that a loan request he submitted was approved and they would like to schedule a follow-up meeting to discuss details. Weeks earlier, Peter had spoken with the bank about his resource center idea and submitted a request for a loan to support his dream.

For weeks, he waited for a follow up from the bank and he was excited when it finally arrived. Peter did not want to jump the gun, but he could not hold in his excitement. He called Ms. Mary and Obie over to tell them about the email from the bank.

They had been aware of his plans for the resource center, and loved to see him working toward this dream. His next call was to the bank to confirm he had received the email and wanted to schedule the follow-up meeting for the following Friday. Peter's last call was to Ramona to tell her the great news. Her excitement was blaring through the phone and in that moment, Peter felt one step closer to giving her something to be proud of.

The week passed, and Peter was one day away from his meeting at the bank. School was wrapping up, and Peter just had one shift at the diner left for his work week. That next day was Passover, so the school was closed for the holiday and Peter took the day off from the diner. His meeting with the bank was scheduled for Friday morning, and he wanted to make sure he went in with as much energy and confidence as possible. Both Ramona and Annalise had taken that Friday off so they told Peter that they planned to tag along to support him as his cheerleaders.

As Peter exited the school to head to the parking lot, he saw Obie and Ms. Mary near the entrance of the school. Ms. Mary's eyes were red and swollen and seemed as if she had just finished crying. Obie was hugging her to console her, but he, too, had tears in his eyes. Peter asked what was wrong, and they reassured him that nothing was wrong. They said they were just happy for everything he was doing and blessed to have built such a strong friendship with him. Obie stuck his hand out to thank Peter for everything he had done and everything he was planning to do with the resource center. He was proud to call him a friend. Peter knew there was something more that they were not telling him, but knew they would tell him in time if they wanted to.

"I will see you soon, my friend," remarked Obie as he dropped his head.

*****

The next morning, Peter woke up much earlier than his alarm, unable to sleep. His excitement was elevated even higher because he knew he had Ramona and Annalise heading into the ring with him for the main event. As Peter began ironing his dress shirt and tie, Ramona made homemade parfaits for the three of them. She knew a lighter breakfast would keep Peter sharp and focused. To Peter, reasons like this confirmed that this was the woman he one day wanted to call his wife. Peter felt that once he was set professionally, his next goal was to continue building their family. He wanted kids with Ramona, and told himself that time was on their side.

Peter reviewed his paperwork while Ramona finished getting ready. She had plans to go shopping with Annalise and wanted to make sure she looked good for her man. Ramona wanted Peter to continue to review his paperwork, so she offered to drive him to the bank. Peter took one last sip of his morning coffee, then kissed Ramona with appreciation.

As they made their way to the car, Peter realized he had forgotten his phone holster and ran back inside for it. Once Peter located the phone holster, he was finally ready to go. They were now on their way.

Ramona made one stop at the gas station to fill up her tank. After filling the tank, they drove into the bank parking lot. As Ramona gave Peter a good luck kiss, she told him how proud she and Annalise were of him and told him to go change the world.

Peter blew Annalise a kiss in the backseat and walked inside the bank. The girls were off to go shopping and knew a tie would be a great way to congratulate Peter on what they knew would be a successful meeting. After roughly an hour and fifteen minutes, Peter called Ramona to inform her that he was done with the meeting and ready to be picked up. Ten minutes later, Ramona pulled up to the bank and picked Peter up.

As they drove home, Peter walked them through his meeting, ensuring he did not miss a single detail.

"The bank arranged to set up a loan that I will spend the next fifteen years repaying. I am so grateful they decided to move forward with me. I cannot let them, or either of you, down."

About halfway home, Ramona passed a police car that was sitting idle in a vacant parking lot. Almost immediately after they passed it, the police lights went on and the officer pulled up behind her. Ramona pulled over and sat with both hands on her steering wheel. Peter, still in his button-up shirt and tie, told Annalise to keep quiet until they were back on the road.

Two police officers made their way to each side of Ramona's car and Officer 1 tapped the driver's-side window. The officer asked for license and registration and asked where they were heading. Ramona presented her with the requested documents and replied that they were heading home after an important business meeting which she believed was successful.

Officer 1 was very polite and told Ramona that she hoped the meeting went well. She claimed that they pulled her over because she was speeding, which surprised Ramona. Ramona believed she was driving under the speed limit, but knew she was in no position to dispute with the officer. She was ready to accept her ticket and head home.

Officer 2 was not as engaging, and seemed a bit anxious with the situation. He continued to stare at Peter through the passenger-side window, which began to make Peter feel uneasy. Peter was not too fond of police officers, but knew Ramona had done nothing wrong, so he didn't feel the need to interject on the routine traffic stop.

As Officer 1 ran Ramona's credentials from the police cruiser, Peter noticed Officer 2 standing next to the window behind the passenger seat and that he had his hand placed on his weapon. The officer began pacing on the side of the vehicle, which made Peter feel even more uncomfortable.

This was also the side of the car Annalise was sitting on, so Peter began to roll the window down to ask the officer if there were any issues.

"Are there any weapons in the vehicle?"

Peter responded that there were no weapons in the car, but "there was a scared little girl" who he wanted to get home.

The officer did not seem to like this answer because he once again asked Peter if there were any weapons in the car. He then asked Peter to place both hands outside of the car window. Peter once again mentioned that there were no weapons, and reiterated that he just wanted to take his daughter home. The officer became more agitated, and Peter knew the answer provided did not satisfy the officer's inquiry.

Peter knew he did not want any negative energy on such a positive day with his family, so he thought the best way to diffuse the situation was by exiting it. Peter told the officer one more time calmly that there were no weapons in the car.

Because of his placating body language it seemed like the officer this time accepted his answer. Peter assumed their questioning was over, then went to reach for the window handle to roll the passenger side window back up. Almost immediately, three gunshots erupted, then there was a sudden silence. Screams from Ramona followed right after. From the driver seat of the police cruiser, Officer 1 saw Officer 2 with his weapon drawn and pointing toward the passenger-side window.

Officer 1 jumped out of the cruiser and ran over to the passenger side to find Peter bleeding heavily with three shots to his chest. She asked Officer 2 why he discharged his weapon. The officer's response was that he spotted a holster on Peter's waist and saw the passenger going for the weapon in the holster.

Peter was struggling for breath as Officer 1 checked his waist to look for a weapon. She saw nothing but a cell phone sitting in a holster. Ramona, who was still screaming, told the officer to call the ambulance which Officer 2 did.

Officer 2 began to panic. He said he *knew* he saw a weapon. Ramona argued back that he asked Peter if there was a weapon and Peter told him there wasn't. By the time the ambulance arrived, Peter had already died in the passenger seat.

The following Monday, Ramona called the school to notify them of Peter's passing. The school held a moment of silence for Peter, which Obie and Ms. Mary missed because they were not in school.

CHAPTER 21:

#GRADUATION

Tremaine Morgan

"Wake up, Tremaine!" his mother yelled from the kitchen. "The weekend is over and I don't want you to be late for your last day of school." For Mya Morgan, her son's last day of senior year was the day this single mother had waited seventeen years for.

For Tremaine Morgan, as happy as he was to hear the excitement in his mother's voice, his true excitement came from knowing this was the day he got to take one step away from his adolescence and one step toward manhood and his future.

He knew a college education and degree was the next step for him to accomplish his goals, and he wanted to do it the right way. Fortunately for Tremaine and his mother, he had no interest in becoming another statistic of the Chicago streets. Instead, his interest was to become a politician so he could make a positive impact on this city.

In his small Chicago community, not many people who looked like him made it past sixteen without joining a gang, dying or going to prison. Tremaine's mother knew that the murder rate in Chicago did not discriminate against age, sex or race, so she worked extra hard to be able to put Tremaine in private school.

The school was a good distance away from their home, but she knew it was the best place for him to receive his education. The commute and tuition was a small sacrifice to ensure her son did not become another victim of the streets.

Tremaine was motivated by his hero, President Barack Obama, who he believed positively impacted Chicago and the entire world. He was determined to emulate President Obama's contributions to the city and wanted to continue pushing his missions forward.

Since his father was not in his life, Tremaine assumed responsibility as the man of the house at an early age. He knew his mother's hard work and sacrifice was what put him in his current position, but that would not be enough to keep him there. Once he realized this, he committed himself to his mother. He wanted to pay her back for every sacrifice she made for him.

That morning, as Tremaine walked toward the shower, he smelled the blueberry pancakes his mother was making, which instantly put a smile on his face. She knew this was his favorite breakfast in the world and for her to make it on this morning was her way of wishing her son the best of luck for his graduation.

Once his shower was complete, he put on his uniform and headed to the kitchen to enjoy breakfast with his mom before they both left for the day. As he approached his mother for a good morning kiss, he noticed her eyes were puffy and asked her why she had been crying.

"You've made me very proud, Tremaine," his mother said. "After today, you will be the first high school graduate in our family, and I love you for the man you've become."

She then pulled out a pin that she handed him as a gift. "This will be your good-luck charm, and I hope it will remind you every day who you are. You are a king, and I love you."

The pin was a golden "1st" symbol, which she knew had various meanings. Mya's hope was for Tremaine to use his creativity, imagination and empathy to create his own meaning for the symbol.

Tremaine told her he would wear that pin all day and would make sure he had it on while he crossed the stage.

After breakfast, Tremaine grabbed his backpack, kissed his mother and headed out.

"See you tonight, Momma," he yelled as he ran out the door.

As he made his way to the L train, he connected with his friend Mike who lived in the same neighborhood and went to the same school. Mike and Tremaine had been neighborhood acquaintances for years, but they became best friends when Mike was accepted to the same private school as Tremaine.

As the boys boarded the train, they noticed it was noticeably empty today. The reason for this was because the public school everyone else attended let out two weeks prior.

The private school year ran longer because of the robust curriculum. They were not complaining, since this was their last day of school. By that time the following day, they would be high school graduates.

After a 35-minute train ride, they had a 15-minute bus ride from the transit terminal to the school. They typically tried to take the same train to ensure they caught the same bus and made it to school on time. They also liked the bus driver, who simply went by the nickname "O". Not only was he funny, but he always shared stories about the various characters who rode the bus, which entertained the boys every morning.

Mya:

For the past twenty-two years, Mya Morgan worked as an executive assistant at a large accounting firm, which had always provided her flexibility with her schedule. Because of her job's flexibility, Mya chose to take the entire afternoon off so she could run errands before the surprise graduation party and to be fully present for her son's graduation. Mya had plans to have a graduation party at the house and wanted time to set up before heading to the arena. She also had to pick up Tremaine's grandmother, who was arriving at O'Hare airport at noon. She was traveling from her home in the Atlanta suburbs.

After wrapping up her morning responsibilities at work, Mya checked in with her boss to see if she needed anything before heading out. Her boss said she did not need anything and wished Tremaine the best on his special day. Mya thanked her for the wishes and departed the office.

As Mya pulled up to the arrivals lane at O'Hare, she saw her mother standing there with a big smile on her face. This was new for Mya, since she knew her mother was not particularly a fan of Chicago. Mya's mother claimed it was because of all the violence, which also worried Mya. She had grown up in the Roswell suburbs of Atlanta and moved to Chicago when with her ex-husband, Trevor, Tremaine's father.

As they embraced each other, Mya asked, "Momma, why are you smiling so hard?"

"Despite how tough the city of Chicago is, my grandbaby is moving forward and I believe he will be the peace the city will need in the future."

Mya was happy to hear this from her mom and knew it meant the start of a positive visit. Mya informed her mom about their agenda for the day and they were off.

As they drove, Mya updated her mom on her work, her future and Tremaine. The two ladies stopped by Dollar General to first pick up the decorations, then went next door to pick up the personalized cake which had a quote from Tremaine's hero. Mya told her mom that Tremaine's friend's mother was also helping coordinate the event and she would join them later in the evening. Once they got the cake, they headed home to decorate the house before leaving for the high school.

As they pulled up at the house, Mya's mother noticed one of the known local gangbangers, Roland, passing by on foot while walking his dog. Mya's mother did not know him, but Mya informed her as much.

Roland stopped by the driveway entrance to say hi and told Mya how proud he was of Tremaine. Roland spoke to the fact that he did not have a loving and supporting parental figure growing up and believed that was an important reason for his lifestyle choices. He saw how much Mya loved and cared for Tremaine and wanted to see Tremaine one day grow to fix Chicago.

Unfortunately, this senior-ranking gangster knew his window for reform had expired, but he made it a point to focus his attention on preventing other kids from taking the same routes he had.

Mya had known Roland for many years, so she did not feel uneasy when he came by. He asked the ladies if they needed any help taking the items inside, which Mya respectfully declined because she had her mother to help. The two hugged, then parted ways.

Once inside, Mya's mother asked about their relationship. Mya explained that Roland once helped her with a situation and they had been friends ever since. He committed to being there for Tremaine and helped keep him out of the streets. Despite his tough exterior, Mya knew he had a caring heart that many in the neighborhood did not understand. Once they finished decorating the house, they began to get dressed for the graduation.

Tremaine:

As the bus approached the school, Mike and Tremaine gave O one of their secret made-up handshakes before departing. While walking into the school enfilade, Mike noticed Tremaine's crush was standing with her friends near the vending machine. Mike told Tremaine that he was thirsty and suggested the two of them go and grab ice teas before first period. Tremaine knew what game Mike was playing, but welcomed any opportunity to speak with his crush. If Tremaine ever wanted to become a politician and a speaker for the people, he knew he had to first know how to speak with his crush.

As they approached, Tremaine smiled at the group of girls and asked if they were as excited as he was to graduate. They engaged in small talk until the first bell which signaled they had 5 minutes to get to class. The group wrapped up their conversation then parted ways.

The seniors had an altered scheduled so after their third class, they all went to the arena for one last practice before the actual graduation that night. This was good for Tremaine, because he wanted to make sure he had an idea where his mother would be sitting. His goal was to ensure his mother got a good picture of him and the school chancellor, which he one day planned to hang in his corner office.

Mya:

Six o'clock arrived and the arena began to fill up with families, colleagues, educators and staff. Per her son's wish, Mya came early to ensure she was sitting in the seats Tremaine had requested for her and his grandmother. Mya also had seats saved for Mike's mother, aunt and cousin. As they announced the names of the graduates, various sections of the arena yelled their congratulations. She knew she had to give her son the loudest cheer in the arena. Mya told her mom and Mike's mom that they would need to cheer at the top of their lungs. Mya saw that Tremaine was next to be announced, so she stood up and began to yell while her mother took pictures.

They announced, "Tremaine Morgan" and the group erupted in cheers. As Tremaine walked the stage, he looked at his mother, kissed his index finger, pointed to the pin his mother gave him, then pointed at his mother in the crowd, then pointed to the ceiling.

Mya began to cry tears of joy because of the moment she finally got to witness. She had waited many years for this and despite the economic and geographic situation they were in, this occasion made all those years' worth it.

After the event, Tremaine met up with his mom and grandmother to take pictures. A few minutes later, Mike, his mother, aunt and cousin joined them. Mike's mother offered to take the boys back to the school to pick up their items, then take them home. Mya had previously arranged this with Mike's mother so she and her mom could begin welcoming guests for the surprise graduation party. Mya was happy to see everything was falling into place.

Tremaine:

As Mike's mother pulled up to Tremaine's house, she mentioned she had to pick something up from Tremaine's mother and told Tremaine that they all would walk in with him. Tremaine viewed this as a little weird, but didn't read too much into it because it was his graduation day.

As the door open, a loud "congratulations!" erupted, which surprised Mike and Tremaine. Tremaine and Mike were both hugged by their mothers. Tremaine then hugged and kissed his grandmother and thanked her for coming in for the graduation. His grandmother told Tremaine how proud she was, then asked Tremaine about his actions while walking across the stage. She asked him what it meant for him to kiss his finger, point to the pin, his mother, then the ceiling.

Tremaine explained that this gesture was used to represent his appreciation for his mother. He explained that for all of his life, his mother had represented more than just his mother. She was his father, his guide, his guardian and his motivation. On days it got tough for them, she always found a way to make sure they were okay. These low points in their life were enough to break most people, but his mother never let him see her sweat and did not allow him to lose his way. In situations like those, Tremaine admitted that he saw his mother as his everything.

With tears in her eyes, his grandmother hugged Tremaine and told him she loved him.

Tremaine knew he would one day pay it back and told his grandmother, "Smile Grand Momma, it's a celebration, let's dance!"

As Tremaine walked around the party and greeted everyone, he noticed they were running low on ice. He offered to run to the corner store, which was only a few blocks away, to grab ice and anything else they needed for the party. He put on his baseball cap and backpack and told his mom he would be right back.

Mya gave her son a kiss and told him not to take long.

*****

After getting to the store, he remembered they also needed extra plates. He grabbed a few packs of plates, a pack of gum, the ice and a few other things. As he began to wrap up his shopping, Tremaine thought he noticed someone following him around the store. His paranoia came from the fact that he felt he saw the same person every aisle he shopped in. He thought he saw her staring at him, but didn't think it was really anything serious, so he proceeded to wrap up.

Once he got all of his items, he asked the store clerk if the woman with the short hair in the next aisle was an employee of the corner store or if she was a customer. The clerk claimed she was a customer, but was also a part of the local neighborhood watch team who walked around the city "claiming to keep it safe."

Tremaine paid for his items, thanked the clerk and left the store.

As he walked home, he noticed the neighborhood watchwoman was now following him. He began to walk in an opposite direction of his home because he did not want her to follow him there. After about seven minutes of walking, Tremaine got fed up and turned around to approach the watchwoman.

He asked her what her problem was and why she was following him. She claimed she saw him steal something from the corner store and he needed to open his bag. Tremaine claimed his bag was filled with items he paid for in the store and refused to comply with her request. She did not believe him and again told him to open the bag.

Tremaine laughed and told her she was not even a real cop so if she really believed he stole something, she should call the people who actually get paid to be police. He said she shouldn't worry about people stealing toothpaste from the bodega and should instead watch her back for the actual crime and violence around the city.

Tremaine turned around and began to walk away. The watchwoman viewed this as a threat and began to get visibly frustrated. She then yelled, "Stop walking, nigger!" which caught the teen's attention.

Tremaine turned around and asked her not to call him that. The watchwoman again yelled for Tremaine to open his bag. Tremaine was now fed up and decided he wanted to call his mother and tell him why he was being held up. As he turned around and began to reach in his pocket for his cell phone, a single gunshot sounded and Tremaine fell to the ground. The watchwoman then ran up to the dying body and checked his pockets for the suspected weapon she believed he was going for. She did not find anything in his pockets other than a cell phone, a receipt, $12.50 in cash and some bubble gum.

A neighbor who watched the entire thing called 911 and ran over to the boy's dying body to try to resuscitate him. The watchwoman claimed he was a local gangbanger who was connected with robberies in the neighborhood. She claimed to have seen the boy rob the corner store and when she confronted him, he attacked her and reached for a weapon. She claimed he threw the weapon away and now she was unable to locate it.

The neighbor, who was a retired Marine veteran, was slowing the blood from Tremaine's chest and again yelled for his wife to ask the paramedics to hurry. He did what he could to keep Tremaine awake and focused on him. As he held the teen in his arms, he told the watchwoman he saw the entire situation and didn't see the boy throw anything. She stated he was mistaken, and was confident that there was a weapon.

Mya:

After about an hour after he left the house, Mya became concerned that her son had not returned. She asked Mike if he saw Tremaine, but he hadn't, not since Tremaine left for the store. She then asked her mother, who had the same response. She called Tremaine's cell phone four times without a response. She then called Roland to ask if he had seen or heard from Tremaine. He claimed he hadn't, but was going to go look for him.

About 30 minutes later, Roland called her back and asked her to meet him a few blocks away from the house. As Mya and her mother approached, she saw police cars and an ambulance, and instantly thought the worst. Roland told her there had been a terrible accident. He informed her that the paramedics announced Tremaine died of a single gunshot, which cut through a coronary artery, causing him to bleed out.

Mya was incapable of comprehending the scene in front of her and didn't believe what she was hearing. It was impossible. Tremaine knew everyone in the neighborhood, and everyone loved him. She asked the police officers on site why her son was shot and was told that there were various statements, but the statement from the shooter was that the boy was a local gangbanger who robbed the corner store. The officer claimed the watchwoman stated that when she approached Tremaine, he reached for a weapon so she discharged a single shot to disarm him.

The watchwoman was speaking with other police officers on the other side of the scene and when Mya looked over, she saw the watchwoman pointing at Roland. A distraught Mya approached the woman and asked her why she shot her son. The watchwoman told her that Tremaine was part of a gang and she believed the gang was connected with a string of recent neighborhood robberies. She again pointed to Roland and claimed he was the leader of the gang.

The officer then corrected her by stating that the police department had already closed that case and previously arrested several members of the swim team from the local high school who were responsible for the robberies. The officer then informed the watchwoman that the reformed gangbanger was not an active gang member any longer and was working with them to end gang violence in Chicago. They also informed her that the only weapon that was found at the scene was hers.

With a shocked expression, the watchwoman knew she had made a terrible mistake. She looked at Mya and began crying. "I'm sorry, I'm sorry, I'm so sorry."

CHAPTER 22:

WE WILL NOT WASTE YOUR PAIN

Oliver Burke

"You see, young man, these are three examples of three great individuals who were taken from the world before their time," the gravedigger explained. "Each of them was committed to using what little resources they had to change the lives and situations of others. Sadly, they were called home too soon and left behind a grave full of dreams, wealth, ambitions, stories, humor, love and commitment.

"I believe, for better or for worse, we all are placed on this earth to change the life of at least one other person. For some, one person is a minimum daily commitment. Others never grow into their purpose. Most people are groomed to believe their purpose is fulfilled while getting paid at their nine to five, paying off debt or running a marathon. As great as these accomplishments are, they fail to truly fulfill any person if you do nothing with what you've achieved."

"Historically, the misconception of our purpose versus our position has been formed because of a lack of knowledge. The two words have been used interchangeably for many, many years, which has made it difficult for people to differentiate between the two when speaking about fulfillment.

"For example, a person who stops by the local homeless shelter if they have any tangible discretionary resources available to them, is a person who understands their purpose. This person understands that the true extent of what they can offer goes deeper than money, clothes or food. To these people, time, love, attention and humor can hold just as much of an impact as money. These people also understand that they are not in their current life situation by chance.

"If that same person was only living out their position, they would not stop by the homeless shelter unless they saw some sort of personal gain from it or had extra money to give. In some cases, even if they had an excess of resources to donate, they may choose not to because it would require them to use their own time. Often, the gains these people seek are monetary or come with praise or approval. In this example, this person is fulfilling his or her obligation to their position or role. I believe you are the former."

Amazed by the old gravedigger's stories, Walter poured him a refill on his bourbon. He told the gravedigger that he shared the stories as if he knew the three of them personally. After thinking about it further, Walter became skeptical of the entire thing. He told the gravedigger that the stories were almost too good and too convenient to be true.

Despite his skepticism over the entire situation, Walter told the gravedigger that he was still very curious about a few things the gravedigger spoke about.

"What did you mean when you said their graves were full of wealth? Out of the three individuals mentioned in the stories, it sounded like Eugene Garry was the only person who had any money to his name. How could Peter Castile or Tremaine Morgan leave behind any wealth when one had to work multiple jobs to support his family and the other had just graduated high school? What wealth could they leave behind?"

Despite his doubt, Walter asked him another question. "How did you know the three men?"

The old man told Walter to stay with him because they would unlock many truths during their time together.

Although he was still eager for answers, Walter proceeded to ask one final question. "How did you know about Justice saving the woman?"

The old man sighed and stated, "I am sorry that the final accounts of the lives of these three great individuals holds no value for you and your current situation. I was not randomly selected to work this shift, in this graveyard, and be at this particular grave at this moment. It was my responsibility to be here for you, because you needed me. You may not believe me, but you have yet to truly unlock your full potential and live into your purpose.

"The stories about Eugene Garry, Peter Castile and Tremaine Morgan are in fact true and I know this because I was fortunate enough to know each of them. I'd like to remind you, Walter, angels do not always wear wings, sport a halo or fly around heaven. Sometimes they work security on Wall Street, clean the hallways of the elementary schools and drive buses through cities plagued with gun violence. You don't need to be an angel to be a guardian angel. Over the years, I've taken on many different nicknames and worn many different hats, but the name I was given from my father is Oliver Burke.

"You see, I knew these individuals, and I tell you their stories because I was unable to save them. It has been something that has kept me up most nights, and I want to change the way the story ends for you.

"Each of them knew their financial, economic or demographic situation was no excuse for why they could not change the world. I see a little bit of each of them in you, Walter. Your love for life, ambition for improvement and your dedication for your loved ones defines what you stand for.

"In you, I see the same jovial presence that I saw with Eugene Gary. He was a lover of all things living and enjoyed life to the fullest. I saw this with you when you visited the nightclub on New Year's. You didn't see me, but I watched you that night and noticed you did not touch a sip of alcohol until you saw everyone else enjoying themselves. It seemed like your joy came from ensuring everyone else was happy. That night, I asked the waitress whose party it was and she told me you were hosting a coming home party or something like that. She did not know for who, but she knew it was something special like that. How you treated everyone made me think of Eugene.

"When I first met him, I was a security guard at the building he worked in. He was a sweet, jolly heavyset man who loved the world and ignited the best of the people in it. He made everyone he encountered better because of the examples he set. He believed his purpose was to show people how to be better, which in turn proved why we should want to be better. As a senior-level employee at the brokerage, it made a significant impact on everyone to see him form and maintain such strong relationships with all people. It didn't matter if he was talking to fellow executives or someone in the mailroom, Eugene made it a point to let you know that you mattered. He believed the hardest thing to do was finding the courage and will to ask how someone was doing. It was too easy to walk by people and not care.

"In the time I served as a security guard, I saw that brokerage eat people alive. I cannot tell you the number of employees I saw running out of that building in tears. Every time they returned, they all had positive things to say about how Eugene had reached out or checked with them to see how they were doing. No one asked him to do it, he just did. That type of care is what I am talking about. It is something that some have and some do not. Eugene and I used to speak in passing about life and work. In our conversations, he used to make me and my situation the focal point of each of our conversations. Can you imagine how that made a security guard working 10+ hours a day feel? I used to think about the fact that I worked long days to protect people who didn't even know who I was. Most people probably wouldn't even be able to describe my face, but Eugene was different. He helped give me an identity at that place."

In hearing Eugene's story, Walter remembered a Eugene Garry he met at the Sip & Paint event last year. He was introduced as a silent donor, and it all began to make sense. Both he and Eugene enjoyed supporting these causes, but did not require any kind of celebration for their contributions. Because of the previous interaction with Eugene, Walter began to realize Oliver may not be as crazy as he originally assumed. He told Oliver this and Oliver nodded his head in agreement.

"Peter Castile's story was a little different, and I worked a lot closer with him than I did with Eugene. When I first started at the elementary school, I was a janitor and he worked in the kitchen. Peter was one of the first people who came up to introduce himself to me. His excitement with explaining the job and students was enough to make me excited even before I met anyone else. For most of the other people I spoke with, it seemed like it was just about the paycheck. For him, his reasons seemed to be more about being there for the children.

"When he first told me his story about not being able to get his degree in education, it all began to make sense. He could not get a degree in education so he took another route to achieve the same goal. The goal was to educate adolescents on the ways of the world and the realities of the communities they grew up in. He wanted to be a person they could count on. The obvious salary gap confirmed just how much it was not about the money. For him, the satisfaction came from the joy in being able to work toward his dreams.

"When he told me how a better life for his girlfriend and her daughter was another factor that drove him, I figured he was like any other male in a relationship and just did not want to seem like a loser to his significant other. It wasn't until he told me about his dream to open a resource center that I began to believe that he was working towards something meaningful. He told me the center was going to serve as a learning hub for children who need a sanctuary. Because of my own childhood, I understood the value of a safe haven and knew this was the person I was meant to meet. As a child, I used to dream about things like this. After some unfortunate experiences in my life, those dreams faded and I would have bad nightmares every now and then.

"One nightmare in particular came a few days before Eugene was killed. In that nightmare, someone close to me was killed. From what I remember, I could not see their face but know they were close to me because of how I felt at the time of their death. I assumed this was just another regular nightmare and left it alone.

"When I walked into that office that dreadful afternoon and saw Eugene's lifeless body on the ground, I almost collapsed myself. I couldn't believe what I was seeing and quickly began performing CPR in hopes of saving him. Sadly, he did not make it. At that point in my life, I didn't have too many people I could call my friends. Even though as a building resident, he was more of a client, I felt like I could consider him a friend. His death came at a complete shock and it petrified me.

"A few nights before Peter was killed, that same nightmare visited me as I slept. I woke up terrified, lying in a pool of my own sweat. The nightmare was very similar, except from what I can remember, this nightmare had to do with a highway or road. I assumed it was a car crash and became very paranoid. In my paranoid state, I told myself I was only going to drive to work and that's it.

"The day before Peter Castile was killed, I told Ms. Mary about the nightmare. As I began to explain, she broke down and began crying. It turns out, her grandson was killed in a car accident four years ago on that day. I had no idea. I attempted to console her and ended up breaking down myself. I told her how much she meant to me, and how thankful I was for her friendship. As we both began to calm down, Peter walked up to us as he exited the school. As he approached, I thought about how much these two meant to me and how painful it would be to lose either of them. When Peter walked up, I expressed my gratitude for his friendship. I wasn't entirely sure if I was going to see either of them after that day, so I wanted to express my feelings in that moment. As Peter walked away, I silently said a prayer for him and everything he was doing.

"Every time we spoke, he always made sure to mention his progress toward the resource center, which made me believe it was more than just a dream. I see this same ambition in you with how much of an emphasis you put on volunteering. You did not know this, but I met your brother before I met you. When I spoke with Justice, he told me about the different initiatives you were a part of, and how you raised thousands of dollars for organizations dedicated to bettering the lives of children. This is obviously an example of you seeing beyond yourself, but there was a certain situation that really did it for me.

"I was told about something you did one night in Times Square, which confirmed my theory about your ambition and care. Ambition for ourselves is one thing but from what I heard, you helped provide a resource that helped others work toward their ambition. This helped me believe you were the person I was meant to meet.

"The last story was not a story about affluence or monetary wealth. The story of Tremaine Morgan highlighted the similarities you both share with your care, love and value for family. Like his mother, Tremaine understood the position he was in, but did not allow it to be an excuse to stop him from becoming the next African American community leader.

"Living in a rougher neighborhood made him tough, but having dreams and goals made him smart. To set a goal to fix a city like Chicago is not an easy undertaking. It would have required the type of commitment and savvy that his role model, President Barack Obama, brought to his role as Commander in Chief. The other major factor of his dedication for a better life came from his commitment and love for his mother.

"When I had the pleasure of meeting your older brother, the way he spoke about you reminded me of the same conversations I used to have with Tremaine when he rode my bus. Tremaine once told me that his mother was his savior, and he planned to one day get her out of the ghetto and buy her a place in Beverly Hills. From what he said, it was not because he wanted her to have a big house or fancy car. Instead, he told me he wanted to separate her from the demons that came with living in the ghetto.

"Justice told me something similar when speaking about you. He told me you saved his life. He didn't get into the details, but mentioned that when you were younger, you helped him realize how important family was."

CHAPTER 23:

EIGHT LEVELS OF CHARITY

Oliver Burke

"Sadly, each of these three lives were cut short before they could execute their dreams. This is why I mentioned their wealth and ambitions died with each of them. Our dreams are the most valuable assets that we carry and if we do not work on executing them, they will end up dying with us.

"The pain you felt when Santina died and when you learned about your brother Justice was not derived from your heart or your brain. The pain you felt came from the fact that you believe you failed them. You believe you failed to protect them and failed to save them. I'm here to tell you that you did not fail them.

"Santina's life was most fulfilled when she was with you. Before she was called home, you made her final days the best she's ever had. She had never dated someone like you, and you showed her that she deserved more than she was given up to that point. You say your brother is dead. Is this something that the doctors told you?"

"Pretty much." Walter replied. "They said they've never seen anyone recover from his type of injury and they were suggesting I allow them to take him off life support."

"Is that what you want, though?" asked Oliver. "Do you think your brother would give up if presented with the same option?"

"No, I don't," Walter responded, lowering his head bashfully. "In fact, I think my brother would have taken me to another hospital if the current doctors were giving up."

"So what are you doing here? I hope not giving up.

"Your brother is still fighting, and if you leave him, you'd be putting him at a handicap to fight this battle alone.

"Earlier this evening, you asked two questions which I believe you mistakenly asked because of how you felt at that moment. You asked, 'How have I wronged you?' and 'How much more do you want?'

"I still believe the right question is at your fingertips. I would like to pose a new question to you now. Who are you, Walter Benine?"

Walter, who was now crying uncontrollably, told Oliver he didn't know anymore. He thought he was a lover, a contributor and protector until he lost the people he loved the most because he could not protect them. He knew his brother was the most important person to him, but did not know that so many other people depended on him and his contributions.

Oliver asked Walter the question again, "Who are you?" He told Walter to think about the stories he heard and ask himself the question again.

Walter just stared, still deeply lost.

"I can't be the one to tell you who you are. You must realize it organically," claimed Oliver.

As tears ran down Walters face, he realized Oliver was right. He was asking the questions as if he was being punished. He had never played the victim before and realized that he was worrying about the wrong things. He thought about the fact that he was not the one who was homeless, in a hospital bed or in a grave. He cried out the first thing that came to his mind. "I am a guider, a provider and a fearless failure."

Oliver smiled and embraced Walter. As the two men stood there, Oliver also began to tear up. He told Walter that he was happy they were able to share this breakthrough moment because they both needed it. "As you see, the right question came from identifying who you are to yourself, which in turn helped show who you are to others. What was it that helped with this breakthrough?"

"When you first asked the question, I asked myself, but was having a difficult time providing an answer that didn't include my job. I kept going back to the work I do for Karot versus the work I do in the community, and I realized I was mistaking my job for my purpose. Although my work is something I've been passionate about, the success I achieve in my professional career has only provided me with the gratifying feeling of knowing I've achieved my professional goals. You helped me realize that my true joy and fulfillment comes from being able to reach back and pull others forward. I once heard Denzel Washington say 'Don't just aspire to make a living, aspire to make a difference,' and I now realize how impactful that statement has been to my life.

"I have been guided in life by people like Justice, so I became a guide to people like Malia, Robert and the students at the schools I speak at. Others have made such a large investment in me and provided so much for me to be successful, so without thinking about it, I've provided that for others."

Walter ended by telling Oliver he believed he was a fearless failure because of a piece of advice he was given. Justice told him to "never be afraid of the dark."

"Justice might have claimed I saved him, but in fact it was the opposite. He saved my life and helped reassure a fearful young man that someone cared about him."

Walter then began to briefly tell Oliver about the robbery in Baltimore.

"That night, Justice whispered, 'Todo destras de la puetra sala a la luz' in my ear when he saw the trauma in my face. He told me this to help address the fear and shock that was all over my face. That day, he reassured me that it would be okay. At first, I did not know how to interpret this statement in relation to the robbery, but Justice explained his motivation behind the statement. Every truth eventually comes out in the end was the lesson he wanted me to learn. He told me that nothing can break me because I am Walter Benine. As long as I live a pure, selfless life, good things will happen.

"He told me not to worry and to remain strong because darkness always catches up to those who do wrong.

"He told me this because I was afraid. This was his way of helping me realize that I was afraid of the idea of something versus the actual thing. He told me that the actions from that day reminded him that I was stronger and more powerful than I allowed myself to believe. That one statement helped show me that idea of fear cannot affect me unless I allow it to."

"That's a very interesting revelation, young man. Often times, fear is the cause of people failing to reveal their true selves. When they do reveal themselves, it usually shows that they are usually more afraid of the idea of fear verses the actual thing. When people use fear on others, it typically is because they themselves are broken and are seeking salvation from the pain of the person they are trying to break."

"You're right, Oliver. After Justice explained it further, I began to understand. The thieves who committed the robbery that day did so because they feared me and my two friends. They feared us because they believed we were different. We didn't dress like them, talk like them or act like them, so they feared the world would choose us over them. They believed that if they could tap into our fear, they could conquer us.

"Since that day, I have never and will never be afraid to fight the battles I feel I need to fight on behalf of myself and others. The kids I encountered that day in Baltimore were scared so they did what they believe they needed to do for the world to see them as valuable. I realized that deep down inside, a part of my reason is because I want to help kids like them realize they can be valuable to the world without having to rob, kill or cheat. " claimed Walter.

"That is very powerful, Walter. You are right: The piece that most people fail to see or ask themselves is the reasons why people do things.

Instead of banishing wrongdoers, some need direction and inspiration. Thank you for opening up."

Walter thanked the old man for helping him realize that he was living his true purpose and how much of an impact he played on the lives of others. He told Oliver that he still had a list of questions, starting with how he knew about Justice saving the woman, and how the old man knew so much about him.

"Have you been stalking me, crazy old man?" joked Walter.

The two men laughed, and Oliver took another sip of his bourbon. "I have not stalked you, young man. My purpose has been to find someone who needed me and help them understand who they are to this world. Fate brought us together, but time has connected us. The first time I saw you was when you walked up to an elderly man and shook his hand at a bus stop. I got a sense of who you were that day," claimed Oliver.

Walter stared at the old man with a confused look on his face. Oliver had a salt-and-pepper-looking 5 o'clock shadow and was not wearing glasses, but Walter squinted his eyes and jumped back. "Are you the old man I met that day?"

Oliver giggled and took another sip of his bourbon.

"I am not that old man you spoke with, but I was at the bus stop. Like the other onlookers, we witnessed a rare occurrence between you and a man you believed you could help. I did not hear the dialogue between you two, but I saw him look in his hand when you shook it with the money. You believed you could help, so you did. Ironically, right before you walked up, that old man had actually just been shoved to the ground by a young lady who yelled at him as he arrived to the bus stop because 'he was moving to slow.' She shoved him aside then departed the bus stop in hopes of hurting his pride. When I helped this old man up, he explained how bad he felt for the future because of lack of respect many young people have for anything. He seemed upset, but told me he was okay and that I should go back to my place in line. Not five minutes later, you showed up with your hand extended. I am not sure if you saw what transpired moments before your arrival, but from the looks of it, it seemed as if your act meant a lot to that old man.

"Wow, I had no idea about him being shoved to the ground. As I was walking by, I saw the blank stare on his face and wasn't sure how to interpret the scene. It all now makes sense. I've never been one to believe in intuition but something seemed wrong. I couldn't place what it was even as I approached the elderly man but I did feel like there was something I could do."

"That was a perfect example of why we were meant to meet." replied Oliver. "It is acts like that which define you."

"By random chance, the next time I saw you was at Beauty and Essex on New Year's Eve. I watched how you carried yourself and entertained your guests. I was curious who you were, but figured you were just another young New York City socialite enjoying yourself, so I didn't bother. It wasn't until I saw you for the third time that I realized I should know who you were."

"Not long after that, I was walking in downtown Manhattan and saw you and your brother walking out of Carbone with what looked like a bag full of leftovers. There was a car waiting for you outside, so I was not sure if it was the right opportunity to introduce myself. Then you did something that surprised me. You asked the driver to wait a moment and walked across the street to the adjacent alley to hand a homeless man the bag of food. I could not see the man's face, but I imagine he had the same chills up his arm that I did. I believe in that moment, I witnessed your purpose and saw how you were executing it."

"While pulling up to the restaurant, I saw the man talking to himself. I assumed he was just crazy until I got out of the car and began walking into the restaurant. As I made my way in, it sounded like he was telling someone about his day. It was as if he was talking to a female, because he kept saying her name. I had a few extra dollars so I ordered two meals for the man and possible woman but when I walked up after dinner, I realized it was just him."

"That's a very powerful testimony. Thank you for sharing it." Oliver smiled at Walter and continued, "The next time I saw you was actually on TV, speaking about the death of Santina. The passion, emotion and love in your voice when you spoke of her showed me how much she meant to you. I remembered seeing her at Beauty and Essex and realized the two of you were together. You spoke about how she lit up any room she entered with her energy and compassion. I wasn't sure if you had someone there for you to help you through that ordeal so I worried for you. Although you seemed composed on TV, something in your eyes told me that your heart was like a cracked glass on the verge of shattering.

"It was nice to hear you speak about the impact she had on you and others. Your words were therapeutic for viewers I'm sure. But something made me ask myself, who was worrying about you. I later learned that the healing and support came from your brother. That day, I committed myself to meeting you and learning more about your story.

"I looked you up and found the building that you worked in. One day, I arrived to your office building to see if I could introduce myself. Fortunately for me, I had previous connections in the NYC security world, so building security let me know that you were traveling for work and were out of town for the remainder of that week.

"As I was about to leave the lobby front desk, another elderly man overheard us speaking about you and walked over to mention he was also looking for you. In speaking with this man, I learned that the reason he was looking for you was because of a letter and gift he believed you left for him. He said that one night he received a letter from a young lady, and the letter spoke about the joy his music gave him and his girlfriend. The letter said that the musicians' story was an inspiring story of sacrifice. The man then told me that he and his wife did not tell many people their reason for performing in Times Square, so they remembered you. The old man told me that behind the letter was a check for $10,000 for *college tuition for the children*. The letter was signed from *an appreciative admirer*. He mentioned he would not have known who it was from if the check did not have the name Justice Benine on it and a Jersey City address on it. When he searched the address, he saw it was registered to a Walter Benine," Oliver revealed.

"After that encounter, a series of events led me to the hospital where I had an opportunity to meet Justice. I told him everything I'm telling you since New Year's Eve, and he told me the story about what caused him to be in the hospital. When we spoke, he mentioned the woman and child who he saved had come with him to the hospital, but stepped out.

"The way we spoke, you would have thought we were long-lost friends who just reconnected when in reality, we were two strangers who were connected through you. I asked him not to tell you I visited or that I was looking to meet you, because I needed our meeting to be meaningful. If we were going to meet, I wanted us to connect in the right way.

"Justice agreed to my request and told me that it was you who left the letter for the family that night in Times Square. He said you told him about how special the moment was, and how you felt the need to help support their family. He never mentioned anything about the amount. He did say you typically signed these types of donations as an anonymous donor or in someone else's name because of your belief in Maimonides' Eight Levels of Charity. He spoke about how you lived your life as the person delivering the gift verses the person giving the gift."

Walter was slightly embarrassed at being found out, but nodded his head in agreement.

"What you did for that family that night changed their lives forever. Everything you've done has been done because of the purity and selflessness of your heart. Your fearlessness and duty as a provider has impacted more lives than you may ever know. I am almost certain you'll never see *all* the results of your actions, but as I've shared, these actions have impacted others significantly, including your brother.

"The way he spoke about you with admiration and pride showed me that you are more than just his younger brother, you are his best friend and he looks up to you. He's counting on you to be there for him through this battle.

"Earlier tonight, you were ready to end it all. My hope is that our conversation has shown you how significant of an impact you've made on this world. Because of this impact, the role you will play in the future is more important now than it's ever been."

As he wiped his eyes, Walter said, "For me, it has never been about the recognition. It's always been more about the impact I can make on others. Because of that, it has become almost systematic for me to act. My mother once told me that the people who act with care will always affect twice as many people as people who act out of desperation. This is why I try to act on the things I care about. You may find this hard to believe because you're a crazy, and possibly drunk, old man, but you saved me from making a huge mistake tonight. If not for you, I would probably be laying in that open grave right now.

Oliver told Walter that he appreciated him listening to his words as opposed to just hearing them. "While I could not save the other three, their stories made a difference in your life. Someone once saved my life, and I committed myself to paying it forward."

Walter is more resolute than ever before and told Oliver, "I know now what I must do…

"I plan to go back to the hospital and be there for my brother. No matter what the outcome, I know that I want to be there to support him. Will you join us at the hospital? If he wakes up, Justice will be happy to see we finally met and are there for him."

Oliver smiles and replies, "I have something to do now but no matter what, I plan to be there with you."

*****

It was now early in the morning and Walter planned to return to the hospital. He didn't realize he had spent the entire night speaking with Oliver Burke.

When he turned his phone back on, he saw there was a missed call from the previous night. It was a number he didn't recognize, but the caller had left a voicemail. When he listened, he heard the voice of the nurse from the hospital who said there has been some miraculous, positive changes in Justice's condition. She told Walter to come by the hospital as soon as he can.

Walter almost dropped his phone in disbelief. He replayed the message again to make sure he was not dreaming. When he heard the second time, he called for a car to bring him to the hospital. Though he was still unsure of what the nurse was hinting toward, any positive news is good.

He turned back around to eagerly tell Oliver the good news, but realized Oliver was gone. Walter told himself that Oliver may have already left to go take care of his errand, and so he moved quickly toward the exit of the cemetery.

CHAPTER 24:

YOU SAVED MY LIFE

Walter

That morning when Walter arrived at the hospital it was 8:30 a.m., which was just in time for the shift change to the morning staff. As he entered the building, he was greeted by the young receptionist who he met when he arrived days before. She remembered Walter because of his dashing smile and personable demeanor. She commented on how different he looked this morning. "It looks like you just came from playing around in some mud," she joked.

When Walter looked down at himself, he realized he was a mess.

Walter sarcastically told the receptionist, "You wouldn't believe the night I had."

"I'd love to hear it sometime," she replied.

Walter was a bit taken back by her straightforward comment, but saw her confidence. He smiled because this type of confidence reminded him of Santina.

As they were speaking, a nurse who remembered Walter walked up and mentioned how Justice began to show some brain activity the night before. He is still not awake but the brain activity was a very positive step in the right direction. She recommended Walter go home and clean himself up. There was nothing he could do for Justice in that moment so she advised he come back.

Walter was reluctant at first because of the long night he had but knew most of his day would be spent at the hospital. Now was as good a time to clean up as any. He agreed and told the nurse and receptionist that he would return no later than by early afternoon.

*****

When the taxi pulled up to his apartment building, Walter began thinking about the fact that he never told Oliver the time he was going to the hospital. As far as he knew, Oliver may already be there. They also never exchanged cell phone numbers, so Walter was not sure how to reach him. He thought back to what Oliver told him about "being there for him because he needed him." He reassured himself that Justice needed him and it was his responsibility to be there for his brother. He also told himself that if it was meant to be, Oliver would be there for Justice as well.

When he walked into his apartment, Walter saw a letter under the door. He figured it may be a notice from the property management office and ignored it. He proceeded to hop in the shower and change his clothes. After cleaning himself up, Walter made himself a quick protein shake to take with him back to the hospital. He was exhausted but figured he would rest when he was back in the hospital room with Justice.

As he began to gather his items for the trip back to the hospital, Walter saw the picture Santina gave him on Valentine's Day. He realized he promised her he would hang it in the front of his heart and in his apartment, but had only fulfilled one of those promises. He kissed the photo, then hung it in his foyer. He stared at the photo for a few minutes then said, "I will always love you." He then proceeded towards the exit of the apartment.

It is now 11:00 a.m. and Walter again sees the letter on the floor but this time, he decides to read it so he can discard it on the way out. When he opened the letter, Walter realized it was not a note from his landlord. The letter is folded into four and is addressed to "The Man Who Saved My Life." Unsure if it was a joke or if it was even meant for him, Walter began to read the note:

I've never been a writer, but something compelled me to write this letter. I've sat in the shadows for years and have watched others enjoy the basic necessities of life. Water, shelter, clothing and food are items that have been viewed as normal or regular to most. They've been seen this way for so long that it seems they have been devalued of their importance. Most people see these items as regular because of the part they play in their everyday lives. I am here to speak for those who do not have them in their everyday life.

I've sat invisible to people who breathe like me, laugh like me, fear like me and cry like me for years. Not long after I returned from the war in Afghanistan, my wife was diagnosed with schizophrenia which caused her to slowly deteriorate from the world. The one person who loved me unconditionally was beginning to leave me.

When she died, I then lost my home, job and everything else that was important to me. When I sought out help, the world turned its back on me. To think, these people I fought for were now brushing me off as if I were a child attempting to sit at the adult table. For years after her passing, I began to feel like I, too, was losing a little bit of myself every day. In an effort to retain the memories of her, I'd talk to her about my day as if she was standing right beside me. I found myself living in the shadows of empty alleys while scavenging for food and drink to stay alive.

Some called me a savage while others did not waste their breath acknowledging me at all. I began to question humanity while also questioning the purpose of my dreadful life. I asked myself on the daily, why was it that I was killing myself to try to stay alive.

One day, I told myself that I was tired of fighting for the attention and compassion of people who did not care. That night, I found a pocket knife that was left in the trash and thought it was someone sending me instructions for my demise. My plan was to slit my wrists and bleed out in the alley. It didn't matter anyway. Whether I was alive or dead, my body would still be invisible.

As tears ran down my face for this horrendous act I was about to commit, you showed up out of nowhere with a bag of food, four bottles of water and a warm greeting. As you handed me the bag, you graciously told me you had some leftovers you wanted to share, then wished me a good night.

When you got into the waiting taxi, I opened the bag to see it was not leftovers. It was actually two full meals you purchased and shared with a complete stranger. You looked me my eyes and told me to have a good night.

For the first time in years, I felt like someone saw me for me. Your kind act helped restore my faith in humanity, which I didn't think could happen. I did not know why you were there that night, but I want you to know that you saved my life.

Since that day, I've started reciting spoken word in Central Park to give others a piece of my art. I see large crowds daily, and their donations continue to keep me alive. I was even offered a job at a local café to be a resident speaker. I never thought I'd love speaking in front of people so much. I end this by once again saying thank you for saving my life.

As he finished reading the letter, Walter thought back to that night and remembered seeing the man's face with the tears. At the time, he assumed the man was crying because of some drugs or alcohol, and figured he would still leave the food there. Meeting Oliver helped Walter understand the value in his daily mission. This letter from this man in the alley helped him once again see how his life decisions impacted others.

He did not require confirmation that his actions were being received, but thought it was still nice to see how it was being felt. Walter folded the letter back up and placed it in his pocket. He arranged for a car to transport him back to the hospital. Even now, Walter still had no idea what he was walking into.

Walter began to think about the voicemail. He did not have many details and was hoping for some good news. All he knew was that the nurse called him the night prior telling him about there being positive changes in Justice's condition. Hearing about the recent brain activity meant Justice was in better condition than Walter left him days prior. He had no idea what exactly this meant, but expected the worst so he was not disappointed.

If Justice was still in a coma, he was planning to sit there with him through it all. In the cemetery with Oliver, he committed himself to fighting with his brother, and he was not going to turn back now.

Walter's Uber arrived at his building at 11:30 a.m. When he entered the car, Walter decided to contact Moriah to check on her and her son. He figured he can help Justice with one of the goals he set for himself by caring for the mother while he's in the hospital. While they speak, Walter offered to take Moriah out to lunch, but she told him that she was already in the city and had lunch. Walter told her he was going to visit Justice, and that he would grab something in the hospital. They spoke for the entire car ride and when the driver pulled up to the hospital at noon, Walter saw Moriah standing in front.

"Wow, I'm so happy to see a friendly face," Walter remarked as he exited the car. "I didn't know if you were going to be able to make it, but I'm happy you're here."

The two of them hugged and made their way into the hospital.

As they approached the front desk, Walter ran into the same receptionist from the morning. She told him that he was looking much better than earlier.

"You smell better also. You can head to the waiting room; I'll tell the nurse you're here," said the receptionist.

As they waited, Walter told Moriah about meeting Oliver Burke. He didn't go into any details outside of their conversation about Eugene Garry, Peter Castile and Tremaine Morgan, but he told her how important it was for him to meet Oliver. A new doctor then came out and asked to speak with Walter Benine. She told Walter that the pressure on Justice's brain miraculously began to go down yesterday, and that the bleeding had completely stopped.

"We pulled Justice out of the coma last night right before we contacted you. We did not see any brain activity at one point which was concerning. We saw some miraculous changes to his condition that we've never seen with anyone before. We knew you would want to be the first one to see him when he woke up. The nurse will escort you to the room," said the doctor.

Walter was so excited to hear the news of his brother's recovery that he grabbed the doctor and gave her a big hug. He then turned to Moriah and gave her an even bigger hug. Despite his excitement, he was still a little hesitant because he told himself they would not be out of the woods until Justice walked out of the hospital.

The nurse escorted Walter and Moriah to the room and left them at the door. When Walter opened the door, he saw there was no one in the bed, which was made as if the room was unoccupied. Walter looked at Moriah in confusion and then began to turn around to ask the nurse where his brother was. Before he could do so, Walter heard a flush of the toilet, then running water in the sink. Moments later, Justice walked out of the rest room and commented, "Well, this isn't the welcome I particularly had in mind."

Walter almost collapsed from his excitement. He ran over to hug Justice and told him how happy he was to have him back. Moriah then came between the brothers to hug them both.

"How is David doing?" Justice asked.

"He is doing well, and is home with his aunt now."

Justice turned to Walter and asked, "And how is Ana doing?"

Walter admitted he has not heard from her. Since Justice mentioned she was in Milan since last week, he hadn't felt the need to reach out. He wasn't sure if she reached out and blamed himself because he had not been on his phone at all over the past few days.

"I have a bunch of missed calls and text messages I need to comb through. I'm not sure if you remember, but I came to see you last week when you called me. Since then, it's been quite the few days. I think I had a voicemail from Ana but haven't been very responsive" stated Walter.

As they continued speaking, the doctor came into the room and asked how Justice is doing.

"Feeling much better, Doc. It's so weird because I feel really good. No pressure on my head. Fortunately for me, I didn't know I was in a coma until I was taken out. It was probably top five best naps I've ever had," Justice replied.

Walter told Justice that while he was enjoying his top five best naps, the rest of them were worried he may never come back to them.

Walter then turned his attention to the doctor and Moriah and asked for privacy with his brother, which they oblige. Once they leave, Walter dropped to his knees and begins sobbing. He told Justice he was close to taking his own life because he thought Justice was as good as dead and he didn't have anything else to live for.

"I thought I lost you. You were the one who I always could run to when I had problems, and the one time you had the problem, I couldn't save you. When the doctor told me that you might not make it out of the coma, I lost it. I went to the cemetery where Mom and Dad are buried and I think I was prepared to take my life. If it wasn't for Oliver Burke, I would have buried myself in the cemetery last night. I lost Santina only a few months ago and thought I lost you, too. I thought I could control everything and the moment I realized I couldn't, I didn't know what to do. In that moment, I didn't see a reason to continue living."

A stunned Justice looks at his brother in disbelief, brought him up from the ground and hugged him. The two brothers stood there embracing each other for minutes before Justice asked Walter who Oliver Burke was.

"He was the old man who came to visit you a few days ago. He told me he came to see you the same day of the accident," claimed Walter

"I'm sorry … I don't remember any old man, nor do I remember meeting anyone named Oliver," replied Justice.

Walter then described Oliver and told him about how he knew everything about them.

"Sorry, I really don't remember meeting this person you're describing," Justice shrugged.

Walter looks confused and told Justice how Oliver found him in the cemetery and helped him reach his realization that he was living a purposeful life through the purity of his heart and of those who benefited from his selfless actions.

"I thought I was failing at life because I couldn't protect you or Santina. Oliver helped me realize that my story was bigger than the negative things I was allowing to drag me down. He helped me see that I am actually living my purpose. Together we defined Walter Benine as a guide, a provider and a fearless failure.

"When I got home, I also received a note from that man we saw in that alley that one night we were leaving Carbone. He wrote me a heartfelt letter about how I saved his life with the food we gave him. If I had killed myself and didn't make it home this morning, I would have never seen the letter, been able to see you wake up, or would have met Oliver Burke. As you know, I don't do things for recognition or praise, but hearing the story about how our actions that night helped save a life really hit me.

"For the longest time, I was acting because that's what I believed I needed to do. Never in a million years would I have imagined that a simple gesture could save someone from committing suicide. I will not lie to you, I didn't realize how broken I was until I had to define myself. At first, my pride made me think it wasn't worth trying to put the pieces back together. Last night, Oliver helped me realize that my pain was not being wasted and you were counting on me to be here to fight with you."

"Todo destras de la puetra sala a la luz." Justice remarked to Walter. "Have you forgotten that? No matter what happens, the night is always darkest before the dawn. It is what is in your heart that defines you. That's what I've admired about you little bro."

Justice joked that the "Benine Brothers" have gotten through worse pain than a little head injury and coma. They laughed, and Walter agreed.

Walter then called the nurse and Moriah back into the room and asked when Justice would be able to come home.

"We want to run one more test, but it's looking very good. He can probably head home later today," replied the nurse.

Walter and Justice thanked the nurse and Justice also thanked Moriah for coming back to see him.

"Going to have to ask for some privacy, little bro. I want to call Ana and let her know I'm okay," said Justice.

Walter and Moriah agreed and left the room. Walter once again thanked her for coming by to see Justice and reminded her they should plan to stay in touch. The two of them hugged, and she went on her way.

Walter, who was still curious about whether Oliver was at the hospital, asked the nurse if there were any old men who visited Justice. She replied, "not that I am aware of, but you should check with the receptionist to see if anyone signed in."

He thanked her then went to find the cute receptionist.

"Hey love, when I was here last week, you made a comment about how my brother has been popular. I'm curious what you meant by that? Was it because he had visitors?" asked Walter.

"If I remember correctly, your brother did have a few visitors ask about him and for his room.

"Was any of them an old man?

"I think there was one man who came by but his signature was so sloppy I couldn't tell what his name was," replied the receptionist. "I wish I could remember his name or face but for the life of me, I can't. Truth be told, the days here are long and we see so many people that we can sometimes miss faces. I don't recall what this man looked like but from what I do remember, he had the voice of an angel."